"Todd, I just found out that my mom's going to be in Chicago all this week with Mr. Patman, and I'm afraid that—"

Before she could get out the rest of her sentence, Todd broke in. "Hey! That means that all four of our parents are out of the way!" he said jubilantly, his eyes twinkling. "That's great news, Liz!"

"Great news?" she repeated, her own face blank.

Todd leaned over to give her a big hug. "*You* know," he murmured into her hair. "What we were talking about last night. You and me, moving in together."

Elizabeth had completely forgotten about their conversation at Miller's Point. "Oh, right. That."

"So, what do you say?" Todd gave her a warm squeeze. "The timing's perfect—I could bring my stuff over this afternoon. Just think, Liz," Todd said, nuzzling her neck. "We can cook dinner and do our homework together and stay up all night talking and watching TV—we can be together twenty-four hours a day!"

"Twenty-four hours a day?" Elizabeth said, feeling somewhat dazed.

"OK, not *twenty-four* hours," Todd amended with a grin. "I'll sleep on the couch or in Steven's room, of course."

"Of course . . ."

ALMOST
MARRIED

**Written by
Kate William**

**Created by
FRANCINE PASCAL**

BANTAM BOOKS
NEW YORK • TORONTO • LONDON • SYDNEY • AUCKLAND

To Telova Carmen

RL 6, age 12 and up

ALMOST MARRIED

A Bantam Book / February 1994

Sweet Valley High® is a registered trademark of Francine Pascal
Conceived by Francine Pascal
Produced by Daniel Weiss Associates, Inc.
33 West 17th Street
New York, NY 10011
Cover art by Bruce Emmett

ISBN: 0-553-29859-3

Published simultaneously in the United States and Canada

Bantam Books are published by Bantam Books, a division of Bantam
Doubleday Dell Publishing Group, Inc. Its trademark, consisting of the
words "Bantam Books" and the portrayal of a rooster, is Registered in
U.S. Patent and Trademark Office and in other countries. Marca
Registrada. Bantam Books, 1540 Broadway, New York, New York 10036.

PRINTED IN THE UNITED STATES OF AMERICA

OPM   0 9 8 7

Chapter 1

"I'm sorry, Todd, but it's really too hot for this," sixteen-year-old Elizabeth Wakefield told her boyfriend as she drew back from a kiss. "Don't get me wrong. I'm really glad to see you, but this car is hot as an oven. I can't *breathe*."

Todd Wilkins ran a hand over his damp forehead. "Was it like this all last week?"

Elizabeth nodded. "Aren't you glad you spent spring break camping in the mountains? Enid, Olivia, and I went to a matinee at the Plaza Theatre every afternoon just to get into the air-conditioning!"

"Whew. I was hoping that once the sun set, it would cool off a little," Todd remarked. "But I bet we could still fry an egg on the roof of the car."

It was Saturday night, and they'd driven up to Miller's Point, a parking spot overlooking the idyllic southern California town of Sweet Valley.

Usually the grassy hilltop was breezy and cool—the perfect place for a romantic interlude. But tonight it was like a hot, sticky sauna, even with the car windows rolled down all the way.

Elizabeth removed the owner's manual from the glove compartment of Todd's BMW and fanned herself. "Maybe we should just head home," she suggested reluctantly. "We could always take a dip in the pool at my house."

"But I wanted to be alone with you." Todd reached for her again, folding her tightly in his arms. "I missed you so much, Liz. I know it was only a week, but it felt like a year."

"I know," Elizabeth murmured, raising her face to his. "It felt like a year to me, too."

Their lips met in a warm, leisurely kiss, the kind of kiss that ordinarily erased all other thoughts from Elizabeth's brain and caused her to melt like butter in Todd's arms. Tonight, though, she simply couldn't give him her full attention. She felt restless and distracted, and not just because of the heat. *Ever since I found that trunk in the attic,* Elizabeth mused even as she closed her eyes and tried to concentrate on Todd. *Ever since I saw that photograph. . . .*

While Todd had been off camping with his parents, and Elizabeth's twin sister, Jessica, was on a Club Paradise vacation with her best friend, Lila Fowler, Elizabeth had opted to stick around Sweet Valley for spring break so she could work on her

2

special biography assignment for her English class. *I picked Mom for my subject because I thought I already knew her so well,* Elizabeth reflected grimly.

How could she have guessed what she'd uncover?

It had all started when Bruce Patman stormed up to her table at the Dairi Burger and announced, out of the blue, and at the top of his lungs, "Your mother's having an affair with my dad!" Elizabeth had jumped to her mother's defense. Happily married Alice Wakefield, mother of three, having an affair with Henry Wilson Patman, the unbelievably rich and stuffy canning-industry mogul? It was unthinkable! Bruce was just in hysterics, Elizabeth decided, because his parents were splitting up. He was looking for someone to blame, and she told him so. "Just because my mom's working closely with your father on a design project doesn't mean they're having an affair," she'd declared. "And I can prove it to you."

The next thing Elizabeth knew, her mother had flown off to Chicago on a business trip with Mr. Patman. And when Elizabeth started snooping around her attic, instead of coming up with proof that her mother wasn't the kind of woman to lead a double life, she'd found bone-chilling evidence to the contrary: a trunk containing an old wedding dress, a bouquet, and a wedding portrait of Alice Wakefield . . . posing with Hank Patman!

The photograph shocked Elizabeth to her very core, and Bruce, too, when she showed it to him. In

Bruce's opinion, this clinched it: his father had once been married to Alice Wakefield and obviously had resumed a clandestine romance with her. Elizabeth, however, clung desperately to her faith in her mother's character. *Mom wouldn't cheat on Dad*, she told herself now as she laid her cheek against Todd's shoulder so he could stroke her hair. *He's the one she loves, the one she raised a family with. Whatever happened between her and Mr. Patman was over. It was a long time ago, and it has nothing to do with now. Mom would never cheat on Dad . . . would she? They'll be together forever . . . won't they?*

As much as she wanted to believe it, Elizabeth had to admit there was room for doubt. Bruce's parents' marriage was on the rocks, and an affair could very well be the reason. Elizabeth's own parents had had their difficulties in the past, experimenting with a trial separation at one point, although they ultimately reconciled. *But neither one was having an affair,* Elizabeth reminded herself.

Elizabeth heaved a troubled sigh and lifted her blue-green eyes to Todd's face, eager to tell him the whole tangled story. It had been so hard not having him around to confide in.

Todd heard the sigh, but misinterpreted the emotion behind it. "When we're apart I always forget how unbelievably beautiful you are," he said, his voice husky and low. He kissed her eyelids, her cheeks, her nose, her throat. "It feels so good to hold you again, Liz. To *really* hold you—not just to dream about it."

4

Elizabeth stifled another sigh as Todd nibbled gently on her earlobe. Maybe this wasn't the time to bring up such a heavy subject. Why spoil the mood? She made a sincere effort to relax in Todd's embrace and return his kisses with a little more enthusiasm. It was nice for a change not to be dwelling on her mother's mysterious, long-ago marriage to Mr. Patman . . . and the possibility of a present-day affair. If only last week were a bad dream, a heat-induced hallucination.

The radio was playing softly in the background. Sunday was Golden Oldies night on the local rock station, and someone had requested the Beach Boys' classic "Wouldn't It Be Nice?" Todd started humming along.

Elizabeth smiled up at him. "This is such a romantic song."

"Mmm-hmm," Todd agreed. "I know you and I are way too young even to think about getting married—"

"Way too young!" Elizabeth confirmed with a laugh.

"But it *would* be nice to live together, wouldn't it?" said Todd. "Just think, we wouldn't always have to be driving back and forth to each other's houses."

"Or calling each other on the phone," contributed Elizabeth.

"We wouldn't have to make dates to see each other," Todd went on. "Every *night* would be a date."

"Someday," Elizabeth said lightly, kissing Todd

on the nose. "When we're in college, maybe, or after we graduate."

"It's like the song says, though. I don't *want* to wait." Todd squeezed her close, his dark-brown eyes twinkling mischievously. "I know the real thing's a long way off, but maybe we could start practicing."

Elizabeth burst out laughing. "Practicing?"

He grinned. "Yeah. Let's practice living together next time all four of our parents are out of town!"

"Which will never happen," she predicted.

"It could," Todd persisted. "My parents are on vacation for another week, and your dad's leaving for the American Bar Association seminar tomorrow, right? That's three out of four right there."

"Three out of four," Elizabeth emphasized. "And I can just *imagine* the look on my mother's face if I packed up my bag and announced I was moving in with you!"

They both laughed, but Elizabeth's smile faded quickly. *Mom's the one who may be packing her bags soon,* she remembered. *To leave Dad for Mr. Patman!* The thought was too horrible to express or even contemplate. Elizabeth buried her face against Todd's neck. "You're right. It *would* be nice," she whispered.

"People say it's a man's world," Mr. Wakefield commented at the breakfast table Monday morning, "but let me tell you, girls, sometimes it's not so easy being male." Holding the newspaper in one hand, he tugged unhappily at his necktie with the other. "For example, having to wear a suit and tie on a scorcher like this. Talk about oppression!"

"You're just a slave to fashion, Dad," Jessica teased.

"We have that in common, eh?" Mr. Wakefield answered.

It was a family joke that if Jessica didn't have to go to school, she'd be at the mall full-time, waiting for the latest shipments of designer European clothes to be unpacked and hung on the boutique racks. "Shopping is an art," Jessica defended herself. "It's a form of self-expression, just like Elizabeth's writing!"

This was just one difference between the two sisters. The Wakefield twins *looked* identical, with the same shoulder-length blond hair, sparkling blue-green eyes, and tanned, perfect size-six figures. Once you got beyond appearances, however, it was easy to tell them apart. After school Jessica could be found doing handsprings and splits with the cheerleading squad while Elizabeth put in a few hours at the school newspaper office, polishing up her latest "Eyes and Ears" column. On weekends, Jessica pursued three activities with high energy: shopping, suntanning, and partying. Elizabeth was more likely to take a long walk at the beach with her best friend, Enid Rollins, and then go to dinner and a movie with Todd.

7

This morning, however, Elizabeth sat slumped over her grapefruit, barely able to muster the energy to lift the spoon to her mouth. "How can it be this hot at seven in the morning?" she asked irritably.

"Global warming," Jessica surmised, blotting her forehead with a paper napkin. "Get used to it."

Mrs. Wakefield stood at the kitchen counter, preparing a big pitcher of iced coffee. Glancing at Jessica's outfit, she raised her eyebrows. "Well, you're certainly dressed for the tropics."

Elizabeth looked at her sister. The halter top and very short skirt were pretty skimpy for school, even by Jessica's standards. "Really. You're not at Club Paradise anymore, you know," Elizabeth reminded her sister.

"Maybe not, but I have to show off my Club Paradise tan," Jessica rationalized. "Besides, in this heat, if I wore any more clothing it would be a health hazard—I'd probably faint. Or melt."

Mrs. Wakefield shook her head and laughed. "Well, here's something to cool you guys off," she said cheerfully, placing the pitcher on the table.

"You don't seem to mind this hideous weather, Mom," Jessica observed. She studied her mother, who was positively glowing in a crisp petal-pink linen suit. "How can you look so cool when the rest of us are wilting like day-old prom corsages?" Jessica turned to Elizabeth. "I think she's hiding something from the rest of us," she said conspiratorially.

Jessica was just joking around, but Elizabeth

practically fell off her chair. She glanced quickly at her father, but his nose remained buried in the newspaper; he didn't appear to have heard Jessica's remark. *Mom* is *hiding something,* Elizabeth thought, biting her lip, *and Dad doesn't suspect a thing.*

"According to the extended forecast, this heat wave is supposed to last at least another week," Mr. Wakefield announced with a grimace. "I hope for your sake, Alice, that it's cooler in Chicago."

"Chicago?" Elizabeth said, alarmed.

"Chicago again?" Jessica asked. "You just got back!"

"I was just about to tell you," Mrs. Wakefield explained. "Hank phoned last night, and I have to make another trip for this design project. I'll probably stay through the weekend." A shadow crossed her face. "The timing could be better—your father will be away all week too. But you girls should be fine on your own . . . this time."

Mrs. Wakefield didn't elaborate, but Elizabeth knew her mother was referring to the last time the twins and their older brother, Steven, were left home alone, over the holidays. Stalked by a murderous psychopath, Elizabeth had had a very close brush with death.

"You can always call Steven at college," Mrs. Wakefield said, her expression brightening again. "And of course, if you need me, call me in Chicago and I'll be on the next plane home."

9

"We'll be fine, Mom," Jessica assured her, slurping her iced coffee.

Elizabeth, meanwhile, had been struck speechless. *Mom's going back to Chicago with "Hank"?* She stared at her mother and then at her father. Mrs. Wakefield spread jam on an English muffin, smiling thoughtfully to herself. Mr. Wakefield read the stock market page, completely oblivious to the implications of this "business trip."

Elizabeth's heart sank like a stone. Her mother was taking another trip to Chicago to be with Mr. Patman—for a week! Did this confirm Elizabeth and Bruce's dreaded suspicions?

"Chicago, huh?" mused Jessica, squeezing the last few drops of juice from her grapefruit onto a spoon. "Lila says the stores on Michigan Avenue are absolutely—"

Before Jessica could finish her sentence, Elizabeth shoved back her chair abruptly. "May Jessica and I please be excused?" she asked. "We have something to do upstairs before school."

Jessica gaped at her sister, raising her eyebrows. "We do?"

"Yes, we do," Elizabeth declared, grabbing Jessica's arm and hauling her to her feet.

Mrs. Wakefield nodded, and Elizabeth bolted from the kitchen, dragging Jessica after her.

"Geez, hold your horses!" Jessica protested. They reached the front hallway and Elizabeth started to herd Jessica up the stairs. "What is your *problem,* Liz?" Jessica demanded, putting on the brakes. "What's going on?"

Her lips tightly pursed, Elizabeth just shook her head and continued upstairs, beckoning Jessica to follow. With an exasperated sigh, Jessica stomped after her sister, muttering. She trailed Elizabeth into her bedroom.

Elizabeth gestured toward the neatly made twin bed and Jessica sat down, watching Elizabeth open her top desk drawer and rummage around in the back. Still in silence, Elizabeth pulled something out—a photograph—and handed it to Jessica.

Jessica took the photograph from Elizabeth. "I wish you'd just tell me what's going—" she began. "So it's Mom, in a wedding dress. What's the big . . ." Then her eyes widened. "But that's not Dad!" she exclaimed. "Wait a minute, is that . . . ?"

Elizabeth nodded. "Mr. Patman," she confirmed in a dire tone. "Or Hank, as our mother calls him."

"Mr. Patman! No way! I don't get it." Jessica peered closely at the picture. "Wow, this looks really old, like maybe it was taken back when they were in college. I bet they were going to a costume party or something," she concluded, relieved. She put a hand over her heart and laughed. "Phew. For a minute there, you really had me—"

"It wasn't a costume party," Elizabeth interrupted, her expression dead serious. "I found that picture last week when I was looking through some old stuff of Mom's for my biography. I also found the dress she's wearing there, and the shoes and her dried-out wedding bouquet. It's a real wedding picture. It was a real wedding."

Jessica stared at her sister. "Our mother was married to Bruce's father?" she said, incredulous. "Mom and Mr. Patman were—" A horrified screech burst from Jessica as the implications hit home. "Ohmigod, does this mean Bruce is our *brother*? Ohmigod, I used to date him. I *kissed* him!" Jessica wiped frantically at her lips as if Bruce's kiss were still imprinted there.

"Calm down. Bruce isn't our brother," Elizabeth hastened to reassure her. "Bruce and I already did the math. Mom and Mr. Patman must have been married ages ago, before she met Dad and before he met Mrs. Patman."

"Thank goodness." Jessica sank back against Elizabeth's pillows, weak with relief. "Wow, if I were related to Bruce Patman, I think I'd jump off a bridge. How revolting!"

Now that she knew she'd escaped this fate worse than death, Jessica took another look at the photograph, her curiosity catching fire. "This is really incredible, though," she gushed. "Mom was married to someone else before she married Dad! She was in *love* with someone else."

"I know. Isn't it awful?"

"I actually think it's kind of cool!" Jessica looked at the picture again. "Ol' Hank was pretty good-looking back then," she remarked. "Maybe Mom was swept off her feet by how rich he was." On more than one occasion, Jessica had come close to convincing herself it would be worthwhile to date Bruce again just because he could shower her with expensive gifts. "But obviously he could never compete with Dad." Jessica's eyes sparkled. "Who'd have thought it—Mom was really wild! She's kept this a secret from us all these years. It's like a soap opera!" An exciting possibility occurred to her. "Hey, Liz, I wonder if *Dad* even knows about this!"

Elizabeth bit her lip. "There's something else Dad might not know about," she said grimly. "I think Mom . . . I think Mom may still be in love with Mr. Patman. I mean . . ." Elizabeth lowered her voice and Jessica had to lean close in order to hear her. "I think they're having an affair."

"An *affair*?" Jessica repeated skeptically. "What, just because they're going to Chicago together on business?" She waved a hand. "You read too many trashy novels, Liz."

"It's their second business trip together in two weeks," Elizabeth pointed out. "And Mr. and Mrs. Patman are splitting up, remember? And Bruce overheard his mother accuse his father of having an affair. It all adds up, whether we like it or not!"

"Hmm." Jessica considered the facts. Then she jumped to her feet. "I still think you're way off base about the affair, but let's go ask Mom about the wedding portrait. I want the whole scoop!"

"No, wait." Elizabeth put a hand on Jessica's

13

arm. "There has to be a reason Mom never told us about this. Maybe Dad doesn't know she was married before. I think we should wait before we confront her. Promise me you won't say anything about this to anyone," Elizabeth begged. "At least not until I've had a chance to get to the bottom of it."

"Well . . ." Jessica tipped her head to one side, pondering her options. On the one hand, this was great gossip. On the other hand, would the fact that Mrs. Wakefield was also the first Mrs. Patman boost Jessica's status at Sweet Valley High or lower it? That was the key issue here, and Jessica really wasn't sure.

"OK," Jessica consented at last, deciding she was better safe than sorry. "I won't tell anyone. But what are you going to do next, Liz? How are you going to find out what went on—or what's going on—between Mom and Mr. Patman?"

Elizabeth frowned. "I don't know," she admitted. "But I'll think of something."

Chapter 2

Jessica ducked into the bathroom that connected the twins' bedrooms, leaving Elizabeth alone. For a moment Elizabeth stood in the middle of her room, staring at the photograph she still held in her hands. Her mother smiled out at the camera, her young, lovely face alive with emotion. Next to her stood the youthful Hank Patman, his arm wrapped possessively around his bride, with a look of utter confidence and contentment on his face.

On the surface, one would think it was a happy picture, but for Elizabeth it was disturbing—and threatening. *It changes everything,* she thought. Sticking the photo back in her desk drawer, she grabbed her book bag and stuffed it with notebooks. She heard someone honking his horn in the driveway. "Todd," Elizabeth said out loud. He'd offered to give her a ride to school.

She hurried downstairs, her thoughts still running in circles. The photograph was out of sight, but she couldn't get it out of her mind. *Just because Mom and Mr. Patman were married once doesn't mean they're having an affair now,* Elizabeth reminded herself. Still, she was finding it harder and harder to believe in her mother's innocence, especially in light of this latest junket to Chicago.

If nothing else, Mom and Mr. Patman are heading in that direction. Spending so much time together, and given their past history. And poor Dad . . . Elizabeth almost wanted to cry, thinking about him heading off to his A.B.A. seminar without a care in the world, while Hank Patman met Mrs. Wakefield at the airport in Chicago. Would they kiss? For a second Elizabeth paused, her hand on the front doorknob and her eyes squeezed shut. It was just too horrible to contemplate.

As she stepped outside, Todd waved to her from his black BMW. Elizabeth tried to smile in greeting, but she couldn't make her face cooperate. She couldn't hide the fact that she was upset. *And I shouldn't have to hide it,* she decided. *I can't keep it to myself any longer.* She'd tell Todd everything. He was so strong, so sensible. He'd know what to do—he'd help her figure this out.

Climbing into the car, Elizabeth launched into her story without preamble. "Todd, I just found out that my mom's going to be in Chicago all this week with Mr. Patman, and I'm afraid that—"

Before she could get out the rest of her sentence, Todd broke in. "Hey! That means that all four of our parents are out of the way!" he said jubilantly, his eyes twinkling. "That's great news, Liz!"

"Great news?" she repeated, her own face blank.

Todd leaned over to give her a big hug. "*You* know," he murmured into her hair. "What we were talking about last night. You and me moving in together."

Elizabeth had completely forgotten about their conversation at Miller's Point. "Oh, right. That."

"So, what do you say?" Todd gave her a warm squeeze. "The timing's perfect—I could bring my stuff over this afternoon. Just think, Liz," Todd said, nuzzling her neck. "We can cook dinner and do our homework together and stay up all night talking and watching TV—we can be together twenty-four hours a day!"

"Twenty-four hours a day?" Elizabeth said, feeling somewhat dazed.

"OK, not *twenty-four* hours," Todd amended with a grin. "I'll sleep on the couch or in Steven's room, of course."

"Of course . . ."

Todd gave her a quick kiss on the forehead and backed the BMW out of the driveway. As they drove toward school, he chattered on about his plans for cohabitation. "I won't make any extra work for you, so don't worry," he told Elizabeth. "I

17

won't be a guest—I'll be your partner. That's it—it'll be a partnership. We'll do everything together! But it can't be all fun and games, you know." He wiggled his eyebrows at her. "We'll keep our regular study hours."

Despite herself, Elizabeth had to smile. "Yeah, I bet. I'll study you and you'll study me, right?"

"You *are* my favorite subject."

Elizabeth laughed. Todd's enthusiasm was a little overwhelming, but it was also contagious. Living together did sound like fun. Maybe it would be just the thing to take her mind off what was going on at home . . . or rather, in Chicago.

She thought about her resolution to tell Todd about her mother and Mr. Patman. Once again, the moment just didn't seem right—she didn't want to spoil Todd's mood. *If we practice living together for a week, we'll have plenty of chances to talk,* Elizabeth decided. "I just have to check with Jessica and make sure she doesn't mind," she said out loud.

"Ask her as soon as you can," Todd urged. "I don't want to waste a single minute!"

"You're so dark, Jessica," Amy Sutton raved during lunch in the Sweet Valley High cafeteria. "I'm totally jealous. It was too hot here last week even to go to the beach."

"The temperature was perfect in the islands," Jessica drawled, stretching out an arm so her friends could admire her deep-bronze suntan. "There was

18

always a refreshing tropical breeze—it never got too hot, and there was no humidity."

"Club Paradise." Maria Santelli twisted the cap off her juice bottle and sighed. "Was it as wonderful as it looks in the brochures?"

Jessica exchanged a glance with Lila. They had agreed that there was no way they would reveal the truth: they'd spent the whole week at Club Paradise *baby-sitting* at Kiddie Paradise and being two-timed by Mick, the unbelievably arrogant, in-love-with-himself windsurfing instructor.

"It was better than the brochures," Jessica told Amy and Maria firmly. "There aren't even words to describe how luxurious it was."

"No words," Lila agreed, dipping a spoon into her container of yogurt.

"They waited on us hand and foot," Jessica continued.

"Hand and foot," Lila confirmed.

"Ice-cold tropical drinks by the pool, huge gourmet banquets for breakfast, lunch, and dinner . . ."

"Private tennis and sailing lessons," said Lila. "Windsurfing, scuba diving, snorkeling . . ."

"And at night . . ." Jessica met Lila's eyes, and they both burst out laughing. At night they had been so exhausted they fell right into bed!

"We were the hit of the disco," Lila declared.

"The boys were all over us," said Jessica. *Or at least we were all over Mick—both of us!* Jessica added

19

silently. "And they were all drop-dead gorgeous. There were so many to choose from we couldn't limit ourselves to just one! Alex the tennis pro, Paolo the bartender, Kenny the scuba diver . . ." Jessica ticked off the fictional boyfriends on her fingers.

"And don't forget Mick the windsurfing instructor," said Lila.

Jessica dimpled. "Of course. How could I forget Mick?"

"Sounds like you two were in rare form," commented Amy as she unwrapped her sandwich.

"The rarest," said Lila.

"There *can* be too much of a good thing, though," lamented Jessica. "I was in such a dilemma our last night there! Which guy should I dance with, who should I let walk me back to my bungalow, who should I kiss goodnight . . ."

"So I suppose you danced with Kenny, walked with Paolo, and kissed Alex," guessed Maria.

Jessica grinned. "You got it!"

As they all burst out laughing, Jessica saw her sister approaching the table. "Sorry to interrupt, Jess, but can I talk to you for a minute?" Elizabeth asked.

"I was just telling everyone about my heavenly Club Paradise vacation," Jessica explained, winking so Elizabeth would know not to blow her cover.

Elizabeth rolled her eyes. "This'll only take a second, I promise."

Jessica started to pull out a chair for Elizabeth. "Then have a—"

Instead of sitting down, however, Elizabeth gripped Jessica's arm and pulled her to her feet. "In private," she added, hustling Jessica toward a corner table. "Excuse her," Elizabeth said over her shoulder. "She'll be right back."

"Quit manhandling me already!" Jessica shook her arm free of her sister's grasp. "What is with you today, anyway, Liz?" she wondered petulantly. "What's so important this time?"

They sat down facing each other. "It's nothing like what we talked about this morning," Elizabeth began.

"Well, I hope not," declared Jessica. "I don't know if I could handle it if it turned out Dad was married before too!"

Elizabeth didn't crack a smile.

"So, what is it?" Jessica pressed.

"I just wanted to ask you . . ." To Jessica's surprise, her sister's cheeks turned pink. "I wondered if you'd mind if Todd, umm . . ."

"If Todd, umm, what?"

"If he—this is a secret, by the way—well, if he stayed over while Mom and Dad are out of town," Elizabeth finished in a rush.

Jessica arched her eyebrows. "You want Todd to 'stay over'?" she said, loading the last two words with extra meaning. She couldn't care less what Elizabeth and Todd did for kicks, but clearly Elizabeth felt guilty. And Jessica simply had to take advantage of that fact. *Liz is usually such a goody-goody. How many chances do I get to make her squirm?*

21

Jessica shook a finger at Elizabeth. "When the cats are away, the mice will play. You naughty, naughty kids!"

"All right, Jessica. Enough already. Do you mind or not?" Elizabeth snapped.

"Hmm, I'm not sure." Jessica drummed her fingers on the table, a wicked smile tugging at the corners of her mouth. "I mean, I'm not thinking about *me*—I'm thinking about *you,* Elizabeth. What if word about this got out at school? Think of what could happen to your and Todd's squeaky-clean reputations."

"Forget it." Elizabeth started to stand up. "If you're going to be such a pill about it . . ."

"Wait a minute, wait a minute," Jessica commanded, holding up her hands in a mock surrender. "Don't have a cow. Todd can stay over, and I promise I won't tell a soul."

Elizabeth relaxed, smiling. "Thanks, Jessica. I knew you'd understand."

"He can stay over and I won't tell, on one condition," Jessica added with a sly smile.

Elizabeth stiffened again, her expression suspicious. "One condition? And just what would that one condition be?"

"The two of you do all my chores and cook me dinner every night," Jessica elaborated.

"Do your chores and cook your dinner?" Elizabeth repeated incredulously.

"A small price to pay, wouldn't you say?" Jessica

grinned. "I mean, you wouldn't want me accidentally to let something slip about these scandalous living arrangements to Mom and Dad when they get back." She put the back of her hand to her forehead. "And I'm still so worn out from running around after those brats at Kiddie Paradise. . . ."

"Forget it," Elizabeth said, standing up. "Just because your vacation was a bust doesn't mean I have to make up for it!"

Elizabeth stalked off, fuming. *Oh well*, Jessica thought cheerfully. *It was worth a shot!*

Bruce Patman slouched in his chair on the other side of the lunchroom, glowering in the direction of the Wakefield twins. Just the sight of them brought all his barely repressed hurt and anger bubbling to the surface.

"I can't believe my father is doing this," he said to Pamela Robertson and Roger Barrett-Patman, his girlfriend and his cousin, respectively. "I mean, I can't believe he's letting Jessica and Elizabeth's mother break up our family!"

"Come on, Bruce. We still don't know for sure that he's even having an affair," pointed out Roger, who'd lived with the Patmans since the death of his own parents. Behind the lenses of his glasses, Roger's gray eyes were sad, but as usual, he tried to look at the bright side. "And we certainly don't know that he's having an affair with Mrs. Wakefield. And even if he is—and that's a big if—

it's not fair to be mad at Elizabeth and Jessica."

Bruce didn't care about fair. "How many incriminating photographs do you need to see?" he asked sarcastically.

Pamela tossed back her mane of curly dark hair. "You know, I never even saw that picture," she said in a nonconfrontational tone.

"Me, either," said Roger.

"Well, I saw it," Bruce snapped, "and it's all the evidence I need. Mrs. Wakefield is Dad's ex-wife and current mistress. For all we know, they've been at it for years!" Bruce pushed away his turkey and cheese sandwich in disgust, feeling sick at the thought of how his father had duped them.

Pamela reached out to put her hand on Bruce's, her bright blue eyes warm with sympathy and concern. "I know how you must feel," she said softly.

"Oh, you do, do you?"

"I can *imagine* how awful it must be, having your parents split up," she amended. "And it's OK to be mad. But you don't have to lash out at everybody. I'm on your side, Bruce. We all are."

Ordinarily Pamela's sweetness softened Bruce right up. He'd become a much nicer guy since he'd started dating her—at least, that's what people told him. Today, though, nothing—not even Pamela's gentle touch—was going to coax him out of his bitter, gloomy mood. "You don't have to talk to me like I'm one of the babies in your Project Youth after-school program," he snapped.

24

Pamela pulled back, her lips tightening. Across the table, Roger dropped his gaze.

"I'm sorry," Pamela said quietly. "Maybe you're not ready to talk about this yet. I didn't mean to sound patronizing." Pushing back her chair, she stood up. "I'll see you later."

Instantly Bruce was filled with remorse. He hadn't seen Pamela in a week, and he wasn't doing a very good job of welcoming her back from vacation. "Pamela, I—" He grasped her wrist lightly, and she looked down into his eyes. "I . . ." Bruce gulped, not quite able to bring himself to apologize. "I'll see you at tennis practice."

Pamela smiled crookedly, then bent to brush his cheek with a quick kiss. "Sure."

Swinging her book bag over her shoulder, she strolled off. Bruce slumped forward with his elbows on the table, watching her go. Out of the corner of his eye, he caught his cousin giving him one of those "temper, temper, tsk, tsk" looks that always drove Bruce crazy. "What?" Bruce challenged.

Roger shrugged, pushing his glasses up on his nose. "I didn't say a thing."

"Yeah, but you wanted to. You're just dying to give me some advice, aren't you? So, spit it out. Give me some pearls of wisdom, O wise and wonderful cousin of mine."

Roger shook his head and sighed. Sticking his half-eaten sandwich back in his lunch bag, he rose to his feet. "It's times like this that people need

25

their friends the most," he said quietly. "How will you feel when you've chased everyone away?"

Roger walked off into the crowd, leaving Bruce alone at the table.

"Shoot," Bruce muttered to himself. He hated to admit it, but he knew Roger was right. He'd been reverting to his nastiest, most arrogant behavior lately as a defense against his pain over the situation at home. Everybody who crossed his path—Roger, Pamela, Aaron Dallas, Ronnie Edwards—had been coming in for a signature Bruce Patman tongue-lashing.

Everyone who crosses my path, and some people who usually keep a polite distance, Bruce reflected, his gaze returning to Elizabeth Wakefield. He grimaced, suddenly mortified at the memory of his outburst at the Dairi Burger the week before. He'd been so fired up by his own wounded feelings that he'd just blown up at her without one thought for her. Roger and Pamela were right; he wasn't being fair.

What a mess, Bruce thought, dropping his head in his hands. *What a big, rotten mess.*

Turning her back on Jessica, Elizabeth set off in search of Todd. As she scoped out the cafeteria, the figure of a lone boy at a corner table caught her eye.

Bruce was sitting by himself, his head in his hands. Elizabeth felt a sympathetic stab of pain. Quickly she looked away, irritated by this new compassion for Bruce. It was almost as if the photograph had forged a bond between them—a bond Elizabeth didn't much like, mostly because she'd never much liked Bruce.

Todd, where are *you?* Elizabeth wondered, her patience ebbing.

Her gaze searched the full-length windows that ran along one wall of the cafeteria, and through one of them she could see Todd, along with Winston Egbert, Bill Chase, DeeDee Gordon, and Patty Gilbert. They were all trying to beat the heat by eating lunch in the shade of a tree outside in the courtyard.

Elizabeth went outside and walked over to where they were sitting. "Hi, guys," she greeted them. Catching sight of Winston's hat, she burst out laughing. "Keeping cool, Winston?"

Winston, the unofficial junior-class clown, raised a hand to adjust the speed of the tiny, battery-operated fan he'd attached to his baseball cap. "There's no breeze to catch, so I'm making my own," he announced proudly.

"You could make a mint selling those things," commented Patty, who was fanning herself with a spiral notebook.

"Yeah. How much do you want for it, Egbert?" joked Bill, pulling out his wallet.

"It's an Egbert Original," Winston declared with his nose in the air. "It's not for sale!"

Todd smiled up at Elizabeth. "So, what's up?"

She extended her hand and he took it. "Can I

steal him from you guys for a fleeting moment?" she asked the gang.

DeeDee waved a hand. "Take him," she said generously.

Bill pretended to pant. "More air for the rest of us."

Elizabeth pulled Todd aside. "Did you talk to Jessica?" he asked eagerly.

Elizabeth nodded. "Yes, I did. But she was far from cooperative." She filled him in on the details of the conversation. "I'm sorry, Todd. I guess it's not going to work out," she concluded. "I mean, think about it. Doing Jessica's chores, sneaking around so the whole town doesn't end up gossiping about us . . . living together would probably be more trouble than it's worth."

But Todd wasn't taking no for an answer. "Jessica's just being a pain," he said, "for a change. She knows how to push your buttons, and you let her get away with it. Well, I, for one, am not about to let her spoil our fun. Go back and tell her we're happy to do her chores."

Elizabeth looked at him incredulously. "We are?"

Todd grinned. "I am. If washing a few dishes is what it takes, I'll wash a few dishes." He slipped an arm around Elizabeth's waist, pulling her to him. "Anything, Liz, to be with you, all day and all night."

"Well, when you put it that way . . ." Elizabeth's body melted against his. Bending his head, Todd pressed a warm, eager kiss on her lips. The kiss

28

went on and on . . . For a delicious moment, Elizabeth forgot they had an audience.

Bill's wolf whistle broke into her reverie.

"Yow!" Winston hollered. "The temperature out here just shot up twenty more degrees. If that's possible." Jumping to his feet, he aimed his hat-fan at Todd and Elizabeth. "You two need to cool off. This probably won't do it, though—it would take a fire hose."

Todd waved Winston off with a grin. Laughing, Elizabeth headed inside for yet another discussion with Jessica.

"OK, you win. We'll do your chores for you," Elizabeth announced flatly when she and her sister were once again out of earshot of Lila and the others.

She half expected Jessica to throw up some more roadblocks, but Jessica simply shrugged. "It's fine with me. Live together if that's what you want. But I bet you both live to regret it."

Elizabeth crossed her arms and glared at her sister. "And just what do you mean by that, dear sister?"

"It's the kiss of death for a relationship, that's all," Jessica replied in a sage tone.

"Oh, like you know," Elizabeth answered, irked. She had a sudden flash of insight. "You're just jealous because we're doing something so romantic and impulsive. Well, for your information, living together will bring us closer than we've ever been!"

Jessica just smiled knowingly, not rising to the bait. "We'll see soon enough, won't we?"

Chapter 3

"I can't believe you're holding cheerleading practice in this heat," Lila said to Jessica on Monday afternoon. "You're the co-captain—why don't you call it off?"

They were walking across the grass toward the Sweet Valley High football field. Jessica had changed into sport shorts and a tank top, and Lila was still in the sleeveless lemon-yellow minidress and matching thong sandals she'd worn to school.

Jessica reached up to pull her hair back into a high ponytail. "We'll probably only practice for a little while," she said, securing her hair with an elastic. "We have to do *something*, though, or we'll look like total garbage at the soccer game against Palisades High tomorrow."

"True, and their cheerleaders are always razor sharp," remarked Lila. "Well, better you than me."

She fanned herself with one perfectly manicured hand. "Personally, I can't wait to get home and get out of these clothes and into a bikini. I'm getting an ice-cold drink and then sitting under an air-conditioner vent until I have goose bumps all over my body."

"Now, *that* sounds like fun," Jessica kidded. "You really know how to have a good time, Li!"

Lila laughed. "What can I say, I'm wild."

"Speaking of wild . . ." Jessica looked over her shoulder to make sure no one was near them. Especially no one named Todd or Elizabeth. "You won't *believe* what my pathetic sister and her loser boyfriend are up to these days."

Lila's nose twitched as she scented a piece of savory gossip. "What?"

Jessica hesitated. Elizabeth had sworn her to secrecy about their mom and Mr. Patman, and about herself and Todd. But it wasn't fair to expect Jessica to keep *both* secrets. Why should her sister have all the fun?

"What? What?" Lila prompted impatiently.

Jessica looked behind her one more time just to be sure. "Elizabeth made a big announcement to me during lunch—she was so serious, it was like this life-or-death thing. She wanted my permission for Todd to stay over at our house this week while all of our parents are out of town. They're going to *live* together!"

Lila's dark eyebrows lifted in two disdainful arches. "Live together?"

"Todd's going to pack up his little suitcase and move on over," Jessica confirmed.

Lila snorted. "They are just *so* out of it. Don't they know playing house is totally uncool?"

Jessica shook her head. "What can I say? They're clueless. But it turns out to be great for me. They have to kiss my feet all week or I'll blow their cover."

"But you just did! Blow their cover, I mean."

"We'll be the only people who know, though." Jessica gestured to where Amy, Maria Santelli, Robin Wilson, and Sandy Bacon were sprawled out on the grass under a tree, waiting for practice to start. "I *could* tell the whole cheerleading squad if I wanted to," she pointed out self-righteously. *And I could tell everyone Elizabeth's other secret too. Really,* Jessica thought, *Liz should be grateful for my restraint.*

"Now, this is what I call a fun practice," murmured Bruce, brushing his lips against Pamela's.

Because of the heat, their tennis coach had opted to show training videos instead of playing outside on the courts. Bruce and Pamela sat in the back row of the darkened school auditorium, slumped low in their seats with their arms around each other.

"You don't need to practice," Pamela teased, tilting her head to one side so Bruce could kiss her neck. "You're already an expert at *this* sport."

Bruce laughed huskily. "It's my favorite, but only when you're my partner."

32

"Maybe we should watch the video," Pamela whispered, stifling a giggle as Bruce nibbled on her earlobe. "We could pick up a few tips."

"I've seen it all before," Bruce whispered back. "I want to look at *you*."

He gazed deep into Pamela's eyes, gently tracing the delicate features of her face with his fingertip. She smiled up at him. "It's nice to be back," she said softly, "to be with you again."

Bruce wrapped his arms around her slender shoulders, burying his face in her hair. "I really missed you. I should have said that before, at lunch. I swear, sometimes I don't know why you put up with me. You're so sweet. Sometimes I think you're way too good for me."

Bruce felt Pamela shaking her head. "I'm not too good for you, I'm just plain good *for* you," she said lightly. "And you're good for me, too. You make me happy."

Bruce held Pamela even tighter. *She really loves me,* he thought, his heart swelling with gratitude. He used to play the field, dating a different girl every weekend as if to prove that he didn't really need anybody. Especially after the tragic death of Regina Morrow, the only other girl Bruce had been able to make a true connection with—the only one he'd ever loved. It wasn't until he met Pamela that he'd realized how lonely he'd been. She'd taught him how to be close to someone again, how to give as well as take, how to love.

33

"And *you* make *me* very happy, Pamela Robertson," Bruce whispered.

"That must've been the world's fastest shower, Wilkins. Are you sure you even got wet?" Ken Matthews kidded Todd in the boys' locker room.

Ken was on his way into the shower; Todd was already out and half dressed. "Places to go and people to see, Ken," Todd quipped as he pulled his faded red polo shirt over his head. "Time waits for no man."

"And neither does Elizabeth Wakefield, eh?"

The other guys within earshot guffawed. Todd just grinned. *If they only knew,* he thought. *Boy, would they give me a hard time then!*

Swinging his sport bag over his shoulder, he sauntered out of the locker room and into the hallway, whistling cheerfully to himself as he headed for the newspaper office. He and Elizabeth were going home together! *"Going home." I like the sound of that,* Todd thought. It seemed so natural somehow. As far as he was concerned, he and Elizabeth couldn't spend too much time together. *Especially since we're still making up for lost time.*

He narrowed his eyes as he recalled some of the wild events of recent times. Carried away by rivalry for the title of Jungle Prom Queen, Jessica had spiked Elizabeth's punch at the dance, setting in motion a chain of events that had ended in the death of Jessica's own boyfriend, Sam Woodruff, in a fatal car crash. Elizabeth had been behind the wheel, and later stood trial for vehicular manslaughter. Todd, meanwhile, jumping to the conclusion that something romantic had been going on between Elizabeth and Sam, had cut off all ties with her. Lucky for him, when he'd finally realized that he hadn't been fair to her—and that he'd been crazy to let himself get involved with Jessica in the meantime—Elizabeth was willing to give him another chance. *We got back to normal,* he thought. *Until Margo came to town.*

Margo . . . Todd's jaw set in a grim line. Margo, the murderous psychopath who looked exactly like Elizabeth and Jessica and who had set out to destroy them all. She'd almost succeeded.

Todd shuddered, remembering how close Elizabeth had come to losing her life, and all because he'd relaxed his vigilance. He had fallen for Margo's diabolically clever masquerade and hadn't been there to protect Elizabeth at the crucial moment.

If we're together all the time, I can make sure she never falls in harm's way, Todd meditated. Not that there was anything to be afraid of in Sweet Valley anymore, with Margo dead and gone. These days, heatstroke seemed to pose the gravest danger. Still, it was just one more reason Todd was pleased with himself for coming up with the idea of living with Elizabeth this week.

Todd stood in the doorway of the *Oracle* office, waiting for Elizabeth to gather up her books.

Jingling his car keys, he smiled to himself. "Let's go home," he whispered sweetly in her ear, and they strolled arm in arm toward the main lobby.

Elizabeth's lips curved in a mischievous smile. "Don't forget—today's the day you clean the swimming pool and take out the garbage." Todd raised his eyebrows, and she giggled. "Jessica's chores, remember? She'll blab on us if we don't cater to her every whim."

"Oh, yeah." Todd laughed. "That girl is shameless. What an opportunist!"

Outside, they headed for the student parking lot. "By the way," Todd said, "is it OK if we swing by my house first? I need to pick up some stuff."

"Sure. But if you want to just come over later, I can catch a ride with Jessica." Elizabeth gestured toward the football field where Jessica was holding cheerleading practice. "I mean, there's really no rush. We do have all week."

"I know, but . . ." Todd smiled sheepishly. "I kind of wanted us to drive into the driveway together," he admitted.

Elizabeth laughed. "What, are you going to carry me over the threshold?"

He grinned. "Hey, I hadn't thought of that. Thanks for the suggestion."

When they got to his house, Elizabeth waited in the BMW while Todd hurriedly threw a bunch of things in a duffel bag. As they turned onto Calico Drive and neared Elizabeth's house, Todd realized his palms were damp, and not just because of the heat. He glanced at Elizabeth and noticed that she looked a little nervous too. *Hey, we're not really married!* he reminded himself. *We're just practicing—just pretending. Relax, man!*

Todd pulled into the Wakefields' driveway and killed the engine. He and Elizabeth both climbed out of the car. "So," Elizabeth said as they stood side by side on the front doorstep.

Todd took a deep breath and shifted his duffel to his left hand so he could scoop Elizabeth up in his arms. She clasped her arms around his neck, giggling nervously as she peered over her shoulder. "I hope none of the neighbors are watching!"

"The key," Todd grunted. "Do you have the key?"

"Oh, right." Elizabeth wriggled in Todd's arms, trying to maneuver the key out of her pocket. "Here," she said after what seemed to Todd like half an hour. She stuck the key into his right hand. "Are you sure you can manage? You can put me down if—"

"No, no. I got it." Todd clenched his teeth, awkwardly struggling to get the key in the lock without dropping Elizabeth. When he'd first picked her up, she'd felt light as a feather, but now . . .

While Todd fumbled with the lock, they heard the phone ring. "Shoot," Todd muttered. This was taking far longer than it should have. As the phone kept ringing, he could tell Elizabeth was getting impatient. But he was determined to fin-ish what he started. "There!" he declared triumphantly as the door finally swung open.

The phone was still ringing insistently. As they burst through the door, Prince Albert, the Wakefields' golden retriever, bounded up, barking excitedly at this unusual entrance. Todd caught the toe of his sneaker under the edge of the rug in the entry and lurched forward. Instead of depositing Elizabeth gracefully on her feet, they both sprawled into the front hall, panting.

Recovering her balance, Elizabeth sprinted into the kitchen to grab the phone. Todd stumbled after her. The ordinarily placid Prince Albert continued to bark madly.

"Oh, hi," Todd heard Elizabeth say breathlessly into the phone. "Hang on a sec." She put her hand over the receiver and turned to the dog. "For heaven's sake, Prince Albert. It's only Todd. Calm down," she commanded. "Sorry, Bruce. You'd think that dog had never seen people before. What's up?"

Todd's forehead wrinkled. *Patman? Must be calling for Jessica,* he thought, though even that struck him as odd.

"Oh geez, OK. I'll be right over," Elizabeth told Bruce, and then replaced the receiver.

Now Todd was really surprised. "What's going on?" he asked.

"Something's come up," Elizabeth replied, rushing back into the hallway to retrieve her shoulder bag. "I have to run over to Bruce's for a few minutes—I shouldn't be long." She was almost out the door when she stopped and said, "Darn. Jessica has the Jeep. Can I borrow your car?"

Todd stared at his girlfriend, befuddled. There was nothing to do but nod and give her the car keys. "Sure, but—"

Standing on tiptoes, Elizabeth gave him a quick kiss. "I'm sorry about this, sweetie. I'll be back soon, I promise!"

Before Todd could ask for an explanation, Elizabeth had dashed out the door and was revving the engine of the BMW. Completely mystified, Todd picked up his duffel bag and watched her speed off . . . to meet Bruce Patman, of all people! *So much for the start of our honeymoon!* he thought wryly.

Jessica parked the Jeep in the garage. Breezing into the kitchen, she dumped her cheerleading gear on the floor and made a beeline for the refrigerator, elbowing her way past Todd as she went. "Man, I'm usually not the sweaty type," she remarked. "I like to think I *glow* rather than *perspire*. But today . . ." She shook her head as she poured herself a tall glass of icy-cold lemonade. "Practice was brutal. Forget being feminine! There was just no way—"

Jessica stopped, looking around the kitchen. "Where's the other lovebird?" she chirped slyly. "Building a little nest somewhere?"

"She, uh, she went over to Bruce's," Todd mumbled, turning away from Jessica in order to rummage in the cupboard.

Jessica raised her eyebrows. "Bruce Patman's?"

"Do you know another Bruce?" Todd asked irritably.

"No, I suppose not." Jessica sipped her lemonade, the wheels in her brain spinning. *Hmm, how interesting. Elizabeth and Bruce! I wonder what they're up to.* Then she remembered the photograph her sister had shown her that morning. Of course—this must have something to do with the alleged Alice Wakefield/Henry Patman affair.

But how come Elizabeth ditched Todd? Jessica wondered. *Wouldn't he want to be part of the affair police?* "Hmm," she said out loud.

"What do you mean, 'hmm'?" asked Todd.

Jessica stared at Todd and he stared back at her, obviously hungry for a clue. *He doesn't know!* Jessica realized. *Elizabeth hasn't told him about the picture of Mom and Mr. Patman! I wonder why.*

Whatever the reason, Jessica wasn't about to keep such a choice morsel of dirt to herself. *Liz made me promise not to tell anybody, but Todd doesn't count now that he's living here. He's practically part of the family.* A crafty idea struck her. *While I'm at it, I might as well have a good time. What a golden opportunity to cause trouble in paradise for the most sickly-sweet, boring couple in the history of the world!*

Todd was still looking at Jessica, hanging on her next word. "You mean, Liz didn't tell you?" Jessica said, feigning shock.

A worried line furrowed Todd's brow. "Tell me what?"

Jessica sighed dramatically. "I can't believe she didn't tell you about something this important! Why on earth would she keep it a secret from you, of all people? Unless, of course, she and Bruce . . ."

Jessica let the tantalizing unfinished sentence dangle. Todd, pouring himself a drink, missed his glass and splashed lemonade all over the counter. "What *about* her and Bruce?"

"Here, let me help you with that." Jessica grabbed a sponge and wiped up the lemonade. Then she pulled a bag of tortilla chips from the cupboard. "How about a snack?"

"What about Liz and Bruce?" Todd repeated.

His blood pressure was rising visibly. Jessica stifled a giggle. "Well, while you were away on your camping trip . . ." She paused to get a bowl of guacamole out of the fridge, giving Todd a moment to imagine the worst. "You sure you don't want a snack?"

"Jessica!"

"All right. You don't have to yell. You heard that Bruce's parents are splitting up, right? Well, it turns out Mr. Patman's been having an affair. Or that's what Mrs. Patman says. And he happens to be spending a lot of time these days with our mother. As a matter of fact, they're in Chicago together on business even as we speak. But then, you knew that much." Jessica pinched his cheek playfully as Todd tried to wriggle away. "That's why you're here, right? So, anyway, Liz and Bruce have concocted this harebrained theory that Mom is the person Mr. Patman's fooling around with! Now, I personally think that's pretty unlikely, but what really has Elizabeth and Bruce in a sweat is the picture."

Todd looked dizzy. He wiped his gleaming forehead on the sleeve of his polo shirt. "The picture?"

"The old wedding picture Liz found in the attic. Of our mom and Mr. Patman."

Todd's jaw dropped. Jessica dipped a tortilla chip in the guacamole. "Umm, this is really yummy. Have some," she urged.

Mechanically Todd dipped a chip. For a moment they munched in silence. "Why didn't she tell me?" he burst out suddenly. "This is terrible! Liz must be so upset!"

"She's devastated," Jessica agreed.

"So why would she turn to Patman about this . . . and not me?"

Jessica licked some guacamole from her fingers. "Maybe she and Bruce are comforting each other," she guessed.

Todd frowned, crumbling a tortilla chip in his fist. Once more Jessica had to smother a grin. It was a pretty preposterous idea, Elizabeth and Bruce comforting each other. But obviously that was exactly what Todd was afraid of. And she was doing her best to make sure he believed it.

Chapter 4

Elizabeth drove along Valley Crest Drive in the Sweet Valley hills, taking in the view of the Pacific Ocean sparkling like a jewel in the distance. Bruce had sounded pretty urgent on the phone, and Elizabeth wondered what he wanted to say to her. She smiled grimly. *Maybe he wants to make some more accusations. Or maybe . . .* The color drained from her face. Maybe he's found some more evidence.

Elizabeth's gaze strayed to the right and then to the left, from one palatial estate to another. She'd find out soon enough what Bruce wanted. In the meantime there was something else she couldn't figure out. For about the hundredth time since she had seen that wedding photo, she asked herself what on earth her mother had ever seen in Henry Wilson Patman.

I just don't get it, Elizabeth mused, tapping the

brakes as she coasted around a bend in the road. *Mom was a real radical back in college.* Elizabeth recalled laughing hysterically with Jessica at the old pictures of their mom in bell-bottoms and headbands and fringed vests embroidered with peace symbols. And Mrs. Wakefield's college stories weren't about parties and proms—they were about protest marches and sit-ins. Meanwhile, Elizabeth was certain Mr. Patman had been just like Bruce was now: a rich, ultraconservative, snobby frat-boy type. It just didn't make sense. *I mean, it would be like me falling in love with Bruce.* Elizabeth wrinkled her nose. *Ugh!*

Still, it had happened; way back when, Alice Wakefield and Hank Patman had fallen in love and gotten married. Elizabeth tried hard to imagine it. In an effort to understand it, Elizabeth put herself in her mother's shoes and pretended that Bruce, not Todd, was the boy who'd carried her over the threshold just a few minutes earlier. She shuddered just at the thought of it. *No, I don't think so. If he was the last guy on earth, I still wouldn't marry Bruce Patman. Impossible!*

As she turned into the driveway of the ostentatious Patman mansion, a trace of a smile played on her lips. Todd was waiting at home for her. As awful as this encounter may be, she had something nice to look forward to afterward. She rang the Patmans' doorbell.

Bruce had apparently undergone a change in attitude. Ushering Elizabeth into the lofty front hall, he stood before her with his eyes lowered. "I asked you to come over because I needed to say this in person," he mumbled. "I'm sorry for the way I've been acting toward you all week. This is as hard for you as it is for me, I guess, but that just didn't occur to me." He lifted his eyes to hers, smiling crookedly. "Probably because I'm basically a selfish guy. So, I'm not mad at you and I hope you're not mad at me." He stuck out his hand. "Truce, OK?"

This wasn't the usual slick Patman performance—Elizabeth could tell Bruce's apology came from the heart. She was surprised, and touched; all of a sudden the unwelcome bond that had sprung up between them seemed to chafe a little less. "Truce," Elizabeth echoed, taking Bruce's hand and giving it a firm shake.

After a moment Elizabeth dropped Bruce's hand and they stood awkwardly, not sure what to do or say next. "Well . . ." Bruce gestured down the hall. "Since you're here, how about something to drink?"

Elizabeth pointed to Bruce's tennis whites. "You look like you're about to head out to the court," she observed, turning toward the door. "And I should really—"

"Pamela's not coming over till later, when it cools off," Bruce told Elizabeth quickly. "I'm not doing anything right now. Stick around." He gave her one of his most rakish, charming smiles, a Bruce Patman trademark, but the look in his eyes was different—

vulnerable, Elizabeth thought, rather than arrogant. "No one else is home," Bruce explained. "Roger stayed after school and Dad's on a business trip, as you know, and Mom doesn't spend much time here anymore. I'd like the company."

Elizabeth thought about Todd. *I guess he can wait a few more minutes,* she decided. *He knows how to make himself at home.* "Sure, Bruce. Thanks. I'd love something to drink."

In the restaurant-sized kitchen, Bruce stirred up a pitcher of iced tea with lemon and mint. "I feel better, having talked to you," Bruce said cautiously, glancing at Elizabeth out of the corner of his eye.

She felt a faint blush tinting her cheeks. "Me, too."

"Which isn't to say I feel good," Bruce went on. "I'm still—this whole thing is . . ."

"Terrible," Elizabeth offered. "Awful. A nightmare."

He smiled grimly. "That's it."

Elizabeth leaned back against the counter, facing Bruce. "I feel so helpless," she confessed, brushing a strand of blond hair back from her eyes. "I don't want your parents to split up—I don't want *my* parents to split up, either. But what can we do about it? I mean, I still can't believe . . ."

"My dad and your mom." Bruce shook his head. "I know."

"They're such different types of people!" Elizabeth exclaimed. "How did they ever get together?"

46

Bruce appeared as stumped as Elizabeth, but suddenly his eyes lit up. "Maybe if we can figure that out," he said thoughtfully, "it'll help us understand what's going on now."

Elizabeth nodded, itching to take action. "We need to do some sleuthing," she agreed. "Where should we start?"

"How about where you found the first clue at your house?" Bruce pointed up at ceiling. "The attic?"

"Let's go!" said Elizabeth.

"Wow. It looks like an antique shop up here," Elizabeth declared as she and Bruce made their way through the extravagant clutter of the Patmans' enormous attic. "I've never seen so much gorgeous old furniture."

"It's all stuff from the old Vanderhorn estate, on Mom's side of the family," said Bruce, running a finger across the top of a dusty rolltop desk. "My folks are saving it for when I finally set up my own apartment."

"Come over here." Elizabeth waved Bruce over to the other side of the attic. Hurdling a couple of rolled-up Oriental rugs, he joined her at the side of an ornate maple crib. "Who slept here, I wonder?" she asked, a teasing twinkle in her eye.

Bruce grinned. "Baby Bruce. Boy, was he a cutie." Reaching into the crib, he pulled out a threadbare stuffed rabbit. "Hey, it's Lumpy Bunny!

47

I always wondered what happened to this guy."

Elizabeth put her hands on her hips, businesslike again. "So, what are we looking for?"

Bruce put the bunny back in the crib. "Souvenirs and things, I guess. Letters, pictures . . ." Weaving through a forest of hideous old chandeliers, Bruce stopped in front of a set of file cabinets. "Let's see what's in here."

Elizabeth glanced over his shoulder. "It looks like old business records," she observed. "What about those trunks?"

She pointed toward a couple of travel-worn leather trunks half buried by a pile of old sporting equipment. Sweeping the junk aside, Bruce yanked up the lid of the nearer of the two trunks.

Carefully he lifted out a brittle, yellowed muslin dress dripping with tattered ivory lace. "A wedding dress!" Elizabeth cried. "But it looks like it probably belonged to one of your grandmothers or great-grandmothers."

Bruce laid the dress aside. Next he displayed a moth-eaten fur cape and muff and a pair of antique, lace-up shoes. "Minnie Vanderhorn," he said, reading the name inscribed on the top envelope of a bundle of letters tied together with a satin ribbon. "You were right. That was my great-grandmother. Oh! Get a load of these dolls."

Elizabeth put out a hand to gently touch the cracked china face of an ancient, velvet-dressed doll. "I think we've gone a little too far back in time."

"I think you're right." Bruce returned Minnie's things and turned to the second trunk. "This one doesn't look quite so old. Let's see what's inside.

"Bingo!" he exclaimed a moment later. His heart pounded like a drum. He could feel it—they were on the verge of a discovery. "This is Dad's stuff. We've struck pay dirt!"

"And it's stuff from his college years," Elizabeth said excitedly. "Look, his letter sweater!"

Bruce drew her attention to the chest pocket of a rumpled navy blazer. "His fraternity insignia."

"And here's the fraternity handbook." Elizabeth fluttered the pages. "Want to learn the secret handshake?"

"The old sheepskin." Removing a stack of documents from the trunk, Bruce smoothed his hand across the top one, his father's college diploma. Underneath were some other academic and athletic awards and certificates.

"Your dad had a pretty impressive college career," Elizabeth commented.

"Yeah," Bruce conceded. "I get the feeling he was a big man on campus. I mean, that's just the kind of guy he's been all his life, you know?"

Elizabeth looked at Bruce thoughtfully. "Mmm-hmm."

Something about Elizabeth's mild scrutiny made Bruce uncomfortable. "Here," he said, shifting the focus back to the matter at hand. "I bet this is full of goodies."

The shoebox he handed to Elizabeth turned out to be brimming with old snapshots. Sitting side by side on the dusty floor, they examined each one eagerly. "None of my mother, although it seems he managed to date a large part of the student body before settling on Alice," Elizabeth concluded with a disappointed sigh when they reached the last one. "I guess the apple doesn't fall far from the tree, eh, Bruce?"

Bruce reached into the trunk to avoid looking her in the eye. "Here's another shoebox," he said. "Maybe there are some more pictures in here."

But this box held only letters and postcards. Again, they looked at them all. "He had a lot of friends," Elizabeth commented.

"And they all traveled a lot." Bruce flipped through a stack of postcards with exotic stamps, mailed from points all over the globe. "Looks like his parents wrote to him just about every week while he was in college."

"But nothing from my mother. It's spooky, isn't it, Bruce? I mean, it's like she didn't even exist. And maybe she didn't." She looked at him with wide, strangely hopeful eyes. "Maybe we've dreamed all of this. Maybe we dreamed that other photograph."

Bruce would have been pretty psyched if that were true. "One last letter," he said, unfolding the note at the bottom of the pile and giving it a cursory glance. "Looks like a girl's handwriting, but it's not signed."

He was about to toss it aside when Elizabeth stopped him, gripping his arm with one hand. "No, wait." She indicated the faded ivory monogram at the top of the pale-blue sheet. "A. R.," she read. "My mother's maiden name was Alice Robertson."

Bruce's fingers tightened on the letter. "This could be it," he whispered.

Elizabeth edged closer and they read the letter together in silence. "Dear Hank, I'll never forget what you did the other day, how heroic you were. I haven't been able to think about anyone or anything else! And that walk we took on the beach—I never imagined I could feel this way. . . ."

The letter was mushy and adoring; Bruce could see Elizabeth's face turning pink even as he felt his own complexion go pale. They reached the end of the letter and he let the page slip from his fingers. "I guess I was still hoping," he said, his voice cracking. "Still hoping it didn't really happen. But it did. They were in love. And they got married."

Elizabeth placed a hand on his shoulder. "It couldn't have lasted very long," she consoled him. "It was just a youthful mistake. Your parents are still your parents."

"A youthful mistake, huh?" Bruce picked up his dad's old varsity letter sweater and unfolded it. As he did so, something clattered to the floor. Leaning forward, Elizabeth retrieved a tiny velvet jewel box.

She handed it to Bruce, who pushed up the lid.

Something flashed brightly. "It's a diamond!" she breathed.

"A *big* diamond. It must have been your mom's engagement ring."

"Look, there are two rings," Elizabeth pointed out.

The second ring was a plain gold wedding band. Bruce slipped them both from the box. Holding them up, he squinted to read the engraving on the inside of the bands. When he saw what was written there, his mouth went dry. "They—they both say the same thing," he told Elizabeth. "'To AR with undying love, HP.'"

"She—she must have returned them when they got divorced," Elizabeth guessed, her voice faltering.

"Undying love," Bruce said quietly. "Maybe now they're thinking their youthful mistake was *ending* their marriage."

In silence, Elizabeth and Bruce returned the letters and the rings to the trunk. "That's everything," he said matter-of-factly, slamming the lid shut.

Was that everything? Elizabeth mused. It seemed to her that the rings and her mother's love letter to Hank Patman had raised more questions than they'd answered.

Suddenly Elizabeth remembered something and clapped a hand to her mouth with a gasp. Todd! She glanced at her watch and grimaced. It had been two hours since she ran out on him with absolutely no explanation. What must he be thinking?

"I've got to go," she announced, jumping to her feet.

Bruce trailed after her as she scurried back down the narrow attic stairs. "Well, uh, thanks for coming over," he said, escorting her to the door and out to the car.

"Thanks for calling me. This was . . ." She hesitated. "Fun" wasn't exactly the word she was looking for. Elizabeth smiled faintly. "Interesting. Definitely interesting."

She stepped into Todd's BMW and Bruce closed the door behind her. Elizabeth rolled down the window and gazed up at him. Bruce tapped his hand on the car door. "See ya," he said.

"Yeah. See ya," Elizabeth echoed. Bruce took a step backward and she started the engine. "And Bruce . . ." On impulse, Elizabeth turned back to him. "If you want to talk, just call me, OK?"

She was surprised at herself for saying this; the words popped out before she could think them over. But when Bruce flashed her a grateful smile, Elizabeth knew she'd been right to go with her instinct.

He raised a hand to wave good-bye, and she tapped the horn lightly in response. Driving off, she shook her head, a rueful smile playing on her lips. *What just happened between me and Bruce Patman?* Elizabeth wondered. *Are we actually becoming friends?*

Chapter 5

Bruce was still standing in the driveway, lost in thought, when Pamela drove up five minutes later. She hopped out of her car, dressed for tennis in a cropped tank top and a short white skirt, her hair pulled up in a high ponytail. "I didn't expect a welcoming committee," she called brightly. "Couldn't wait to see me again, could you?"

Bruce blinked. On the contrary, in all the excitement of searching the attic with Elizabeth, he'd completely forgotten that Pamela was coming over. It was a good thing Elizabeth left when she did. "Uh . . . yeah. How're you doing?"

"Just great." Pamela kissed him lightly on the lips. "Ready to work up a sweat?" she asked, slipping an arm around his waist. "It won't be hard on a day like this," Bruce said somewhat distractedly.

Snagging a tennis racket and a fresh can of

balls, Bruce escorted Pamela to the court set into the hillside below the mansion. They took sides and started hitting balls.

Forehand, backhand, overhead smash, volley at net—as always, Bruce couldn't help admiring the graceful, powerful technique that had made Pamela, a transfer student from Big Mesa, the new star of the Sweet Valley High girls' tennis team. *Of course, if we play for real, I beat her every time. Still*, he thought, smashing a backhand to the baseline, *she gives me a run for my money.*

"I almost didn't make it over here," Pamela shouted, returning Bruce's backhand with ease. "You wouldn't believe what's going on at Project Youth!"

"What's going on at Project Youth?" Bruce asked.

"You know what the economy's like these days. Well, the Center just found out that they're going to have to drastically cut their budget because of a reduction in state funding. A whole bunch of Project Youth programs, including my program, After-School School, may get the ax." Pamela swiped hard at a cross-court forehand. "It's just not right," she declared passionately. "Project Youth provides really important services that a lot of people depend on!"

"Somebody's got to do something," Bruce remarked.

"Yes, but what?" Pamela shook her head as she missed a shot. "What can you do without money?"

"Not much. How about a few games?"

Pamela served the first and won, edging Bruce

out after going to deuce three times. Bruce won the next two games, holding his serve and then breaking hers. "Time for a breather," he declared, dropping his racket and heading for the bench on the sidelines.

He dropped onto the bench, drained. Pamela sat down beside him, wiping her forehead with a towel. "Which of us came up with the brilliant idea of playing tennis on a day like today?" Bruce asked, leaning his head back against the fence.

"I don't know," Pamela answered, uncapping a bottle of spring water. Tilting her head back, she swallowed thirstily. "The air's so hot and humid, it's like running around in a suit of armor."

"Let's cut the set short." Bruce took a swig from the bottle. "One more game, winner takes all."

Pamela smiled flirtatiously. "Winner takes all what?"

As usual, Pamela's big, beautiful blue eyes had a dizzying effect on him. Bruce ran a finger down her cheek and lightly across her lips. "Winner takes . . . the first dive into the pool," he teased.

Pamela kissed the palm of his hand. "A swim would feel great," she admitted. But her expression was more somber than her words.

"Hey, Pamela, for someone who's having a good time, you look awfully depressed," Bruce observed.

"I'm sorry, Bruce. I just can't stop worrying about Project Youth! But let's talk about something else. Please. How was the rest of your afternoon?"

Bruce thought about Elizabeth and their venture into the attic. For some inexplicable reason, he felt guilty about it. "I—uh, I didn't do much after practice. I talked to Elizabeth Wakefield for a while," he said, making it sound as though it had been over the phone. He didn't mention her visit, or the trunk in the attic. *That's our secret,* Bruce thought. *Mine and Elizabeth's secret.* "I apologized to her for being such a jerk to her about my dad and her mom."

"Good for you," Pamela praised, kissing him on his forehead. "I'm sure she appreciated it. She's really nice, isn't she?"

Bruce's head filled with lots of other adjectives that described Elizabeth. Sweet, perceptive, gentle, honest, beautiful. Incredibly beautiful. Gorgeous, in fact. "Yeah, she's nice," Bruce mumbled, mopping the sweat from his forehead.

"I'm glad you cleared the air between the two of you," Pamela said cheerfully.

Bruce stared straight ahead across the tennis court, a pensive expression on his face. "Yeah, me too."

Returning home from Bruce's, Elizabeth tripped over Todd's duffel bag in the front hall. *But where's Todd?* she wondered, peeking into the family room and then the kitchen. *It's too hot to sit outside, isn't it?*

Nope. There was Todd by the pool. Elizabeth opened the sliding glass door and stepped out onto the patio. "I am *so* sorry," she exclaimed, hurrying to his side. "I had no idea that it was going to take so long! I was . . ." Stopping by Todd's lounge chair, Elizabeth put a hand to her face, suddenly feeling hot and flustered. *What should I say? Where should I start?* "It's such a long story, I don't know—"

"Why didn't you tell me about your mother and Mr. Patman?" Todd interrupted, folding his arms across his chest and glaring up at her.

Elizabeth's jaw dropped. "My mother and— How did you—?" she stuttered.

"Jessica assumed I already knew. Why didn't you tell me?" he repeated. "Didn't you think I'd care? Didn't you think I'd want to help? That I'd want to be there for you?"

It was clear from his tone that Todd was hurt and more than a little miffed. Elizabeth stared down at him, her cheeks turning pinker by the second. "I tried to tell you," she defended herself. "I started to tell you a couple of nights ago and again this morning, but . . ." Her voice trailed off weakly. Her excuses sounded lame because they were. Elizabeth sat down on the edge of Todd's chair, her expression penitent. "I was going to tell you tonight, when we were alone," she assured him. "I do need your help."

Leaning forward, Todd wrapped his arms around Elizabeth, pulling her down onto the chaise with him. "I want you to know that I'll always be here for you," he said huskily. "I want us to be able to share everything with each other, Liz—the good *and* the bad. This is a partnership. You can count on me." He nuzzled her neck.

"I know," she said softly.

For a moment they lay quietly in each other's arms. Then Elizabeth filled Todd in on what she and Bruce had discovered in Bruce's attic. "The rings prove it, beyond a doubt. They were definitely married. But she was pretty young. It couldn't have lasted long, either, because I know she started dating my dad when she was still in college."

"Think about that," said Todd, "getting married and divorced while you're still in college!"

Elizabeth tried to imagine it, and suddenly realized it wasn't all that hard to put herself in her mother's shoes. After all, she and Todd were pretending to be married at that very moment!

"Maybe they thought they were ready for a lifelong commitment," she mused aloud, "but they took on more than they could handle."

"I guess that was it," Todd agreed. "Speaking of your mom, there was a message from her on the answering machine. She left her phone number at the hotel in Chicago—Jessica wrote it down."

"I'm glad she got there safely," Elizabeth murmured. *Though I wish she'd never left!* she added to herself.

Todd and Elizabeth watched the setting sun glitter on the surface of the swimming pool. As much as she tried to relax in Todd's embrace, Elizabeth found her thoughts drifting back to the

59

subject of her mother and Mr. Patman.

"It's wrong, all wrong," she said out loud. "Mom should be home with her family, not off on a business trip that's probably just a cover for . . ." Elizabeth squeezed her eyes shut, unable to finish the sentence.

Todd held on to her tightly. "Go ahead, Elizabeth. Let it out. I'm here for you," he reminded her. "And I won't leave you." Elizabeth nodded wordlessly, in her mind's eye seeing Todd's duffel bag in the front hallway.

"What a perfect evening," Todd remarked with satisfaction as he and Elizabeth curled up on the den couch that night after walking Prince Albert.

"Mmm," murmured Elizabeth. "Dinner was great. Thanks."

Propping his back up against a pillow, Todd cradled Elizabeth in his arms. "I think I could get used to this living-together thing. We've struck a nice balance, don't you think? We went out for ice cream and now we're watching some TV, but we did our homework first. Pretty mature and responsible of us, eh?"

"We're too good to be true," Elizabeth kidded.

"Yep, we got off to a rough start this afternoon, but we're on track now," Todd concluded. The irritation he'd felt when Elizabeth dashed off to see Bruce, and the surprise of learning that she hadn't confided in him about her mother and Mr.

Patman, had faded away. "This is going to be the best week of our lives, Liz."

He shifted his position on the sofa, turning his body to face Elizabeth's. Just as they brought their mouths together in a kiss, Jessica breezed into the family room.

She cleared her throat loudly, and Todd and Elizabeth jumped apart. "Just wanted to say good night," Jessica announced.

"Good night," Todd replied, preparing to resume kissing Elizabeth as soon as he heard Jessica's footsteps on the stairs.

Jessica didn't appear in a hurry to leave, however. "This is probably a good time to place my order for breakfast tomorrow morning," she added, leaning against the door frame.

"How can you think about breakfast when you just ate twenty pounds of tortellini and a gallon of ice cream?" Elizabeth asked incredulously.

Jessica ignored her. "I have a serious craving for . . . French toast," she declared.

"French toast, in this heat? You're crazy!" scoffed Elizabeth. "You can eat cold cereal and fruit like the rest of us."

"French toast," Jessica repeated stubbornly, folding her arms across her chest. "French toast, or by homeroom everybody at Sweet Valley High will know you two are living together."

Todd felt Elizabeth's body tense; she was gearing up for battle. "French toast it is," he said with a grin before a shouting match could develop. "No problem, Jessica. Service with a smile, right, Liz?"

Elizabeth scowled, and Todd gave her a squeeze. "Remember, every little favor we do for Jessica is really a favor to ourselves," he whispered in her ear.

Elizabeth sighed. "Fine. We'll make French toast," she mumbled.

"Thanks, guys. Don't let the bedbugs bite." Jessica moved her eyebrows up and down, then turned and bounced out of the room.

At that moment the phone rang. Todd started to reach for it, then pulled back his hand. "Oops," he said. "Could be your parents."

Stretching an arm toward the phone on the end table, Elizabeth picked up the receiver. "Hello? Oh, hi, Penny. What's up?"

Todd watched Elizabeth listen to Penny's reply. "Really? Wow, that's a bummer. Sure, I can make it," she said, nodding. "See you then. Bye."

She hung up the phone and gave Todd an apologetic look. "That was Penny," Elizabeth explained. "The paper's supposed to go to press tomorrow, but there was a problem with the computer, so she's calling an emergency staff meeting before school." Elizabeth grimaced. "Seven thirty."

"I'll drive you," Todd offered.

"Thanks, but I'll call Olivia and see if she can pick me up on her way. Jessica wants French toast, remember? Unfortunately, you'll be on your own in the service-with-a-smile department," Elizabeth

62

said wryly. "Think you can you handle it?"

"Are you kidding?" said Todd, just a bit disappointed that he and Elizabeth wouldn't be whipping up a gourmet breakfast together. "It'll be a snap!"

Much later Elizabeth wriggled in Todd's arms, shifting her position on the couch so she could check the time. "I think it's getting late," she whispered as she peered at the clock on the den wall. "Correction: I *know* it's getting late."

Todd pulled her back down on the sofa. "Just one more kiss," he murmured.

Elizabeth laughed. "That's what you said an hour ago, and we're still here!"

He grinned, sliding a hand around the back of her neck and bringing her face close to his. "Just one . . . more . . ."

Todd's lips met hers in a warm, sweet, lingering kiss. With a sigh of pleasure, Elizabeth melted against him, her willpower vanquished. "We'll pay for this tomorrow, you know," she murmured, rubbing his shoulders.

"I don't care," Todd said.

Fifteen minutes later, Elizabeth disentangled herself from Todd's embrace. "This time I mean it," she said with a sleepy smile. "I'm not tired of this, but I am tired. And it is only Monday," she reminded him. She glanced at the clock again. "Well, Tuesday. Whatever. We have five more nights together!"

Todd kissed Elizabeth's nose. "It's my wildest dream come true."

Climbing to their feet, they shuffled into the front hallway. At the bottom of the stairs, Elizabeth stood on tiptoes to give Todd a final good-night kiss. "Are you sure you wouldn't be more comfortable in Steven's room?" she asked. Her older brother, a freshman at Sweet Valley University, had his own apartment.

"The pull-out couch is fine," Todd assured her. "This way you and Jessica have more privacy, and I won't be tempted to barge into your room for a early-morning pillow fight."

"See you in the morning," Elizabeth said, smiling.

"Sweet dreams."

A few minutes later Elizabeth had washed up and changed into her nightgown. Sitting on the edge of her bed, she set the alarm on her clock radio. *I stayed up three hours later than usual, and I have to get up an hour earlier because of the* Oracle *meeting,* she thought, yawning. *Ouch, is that going to hurt!*

Pulling back the covers, Elizabeth plumped up her pillow, thrilled at the prospect of lying down and closing her eyes. Instead of climbing into bed, however, she walked across the room toward her desk. Opening the top drawer, she removed the photograph of her mother and Mr. Patman.

Mom . . . Elizabeth stared at the picture, trying hard to focus her sleepy eyes. *What were you thinking back then? What were you feeling? Who were you?*

The young bride in the photograph just smiled, eternally silent and inscrutable. Still hoping for some kind of answer, some kind of intuitive feeling, Elizabeth gazed at the picture until her vision grew blurry from fatigue. The fair-haired girl and dark-haired boy in the photograph seemed to waver, to dissolve and change. For a split second, the faces Elizabeth saw weren't Hank's and Alice's, but Bruce's and her own.

"No!" Elizabeth whispered, startled back into wakefulness. She shoved the photograph back into the desk drawer and jumped into bed, turning out the light and pulling up the covers in one swift motion.

Maybe someday I'll stand next to Todd in a long white wedding dress, Elizabeth thought, *but never next to Bruce.*

Ugh. I could never marry Bruce. I love Todd, she told herself as she started to doze off. *I love Todd, not Bruce, not Bruce, Bruce, Bruce. . . .*

Chapter 6

Elizabeth burst into the kitchen early Tuesday morning just as Olivia started honking. Whipping open the refrigerator, she grabbed an apple, then spun back around to give Todd a quick good-bye kiss. "Sorry I can't stay for breakfast," she called as she dashed out the door. "See you at school!"

The door slammed behind her. Slumping against the counter, Todd yawned widely, rubbing his still-sleepy eyes. "What're the odds that Jess'll wake up and decide she'll just have a yogurt for breakfast?" he mumbled out loud to himself.

"Not very good," Jessica said cheerfully, flouncing into the kitchen in her bathrobe and bare feet. "I dreamed about French toast last night. French toast with a side of bacon, and a slice of cantaloupe, and a glass of fresh-squeezed orange juice . . ."

"Give me a break," Todd groaned. "I'm not a short-order cook."

Jessica plopped down in a chair, grinning. "This week you are!"

"Well, there probably isn't any bacon," Todd said hopefully.

"Top shelf, on the left," Jessica directed. "And I like mine extra crispy."

With a grouchy sigh, Todd pulled out the package of bacon. Hunting up a skillet, he tossed in a few slices and turned on the stove. Then he grabbed a cookbook from the shelf, flipping to the index. "Hmm, French toast," he mumbled, scanning the recipe. "Bread, eggs, milk . . . looks easy enough."

Jessica was drumming her fingers on the counter. "How about that juice? Make it a big glass—it's hot and I'm thirsty."

Todd gave her an exaggeratedly ingratiating smile. "Coming right up, *madame*."

Slicing a few juice oranges in half, he pressed them one at a time on the electric juicer. When the glass was full, he bowed and presented it to Jessica.

Holding the glass up to the light, she inspected it with a fastidious frown. "There are seeds in here," she complained. "And way too much pulp. Would you strain it, please?"

Todd glared at Jessica. She smiled back angelically. "You're so nice to cook me breakfast, Todd. And everyone would agree, if I were to tell them about this, which of course I won't unless you force me to by making me drink seedy, pulpy orange juice."

Snatching the glass back from Jessica, Todd strained the juice and returned it to her. He checked the bacon, which had started to sizzle. "OK," he said, rubbing his hands together. "French toast. I need bread."

Sipping her juice, Jessica pointed to the cupboard. "In there. I'd like whole wheat, please."

"Your wish is my command." Todd dumped half a loaf of whole-wheat bread onto a plate. Choosing a medium-sized mixing bowl, he cracked half a dozen eggs into it and added a few cups of milk. "Do you think this will be enough?" he asked.

Jessica smothered a grin. "Probably. Oh, and Todd, maybe you should check the bacon."

Turning quickly, Todd grabbed a fork to flip the fast-browning bacon onto the other side. "I'll give it a few more minutes. You said extra crispy, right?"

"Right."

Lifting an arm, Todd blotted his forehead on the sleeve of his T-shirt. The kitchen was starting to heat up, and so was he. He wedged the slices of bread into the mixing bowl, pressing down on them with a wooden spoon so they'd soak up the liquid. "I'll just stir this up a little."

Jessica giggled. Todd narrowed his eyes at her. "What's the problem?" he inquired testily. "Do you have something to say?"

"Oh, no." She smiled. "I just never saw anyone stir French toast before."

"It's a time-honored culinary technique," Todd retorted. "All the great chefs stir their French toast. OK, let's heat up another skillet, melt some butter. Here we go!"

Reaching into the mixing bowl, he lifted out a piece of dripping bread with his fingertips. The bread fell to pieces, most of it plopping back into the bowl. Jessica laughed; Todd grimaced. *Hmm, maybe stirring it was a mistake,* he thought. *I'll be darned if I'll admit it to Jessica, though!*

"Just testing to see if it's ready for the pan, and it is," he pronounced with false assurance. "And the utensil of choice is . . . a slotted spoon." Ladling up the soggy chunks of bread, he dumped them into the hot frying pan. "Yum, doesn't that look good?"

Jessica wrinkled her nose, looking dubious. "Yeah, absolutely delicious."

Todd poked at the mess in the frying pan. "It's going to taste great," he promised her without much conviction. "With some maple syrup on top . . ."

He turned away from the stove and opened the fridge. Bending to reach for the syrup, he closed his eyes for a moment, enjoying the blast of cold air on his face. When Jessica shrieked, he jumped, dropping the syrup bottle on the floor.

"The bacon!" she cried, pointing toward the stove.

A startling black cloud rose from the skillet. Todd rushed to the stove, waving the smoke away

69

from his face and coughing. Just then the smoke alarm went off, blaring through the house like an ambulance siren.

Using a hot mitt, Todd snatched the skillet of burning bacon and hurled it into the sink, turning on the cold water full blast. Steam billowed up, hissing madly. "Bacon on the side," Todd snapped. "You just had to have bacon on the side, didn't you?"

Jessica was doubled over, laughing hysterically as she went to turn off the smoke alarm. "How was I supposed to know you were going to burn the whole house down, trying to make it?"

Todd stomped back to the stove to inspect the French toast. The puddle of soggy bread chunks bubbled halfheartedly in the other pan. "So, how's the French toast coming?" Jessica asked, returning to look over Todd's shoulder and bursting into laughter again.

"Just forget it, okay?" Todd hurled the botched French toast into the garbage, along with the last shred of his patience. "You can go to the Dairi Burger for breakfast and harass *their* cook!"

Jessica was still laughing helplessly as he grabbed his wallet, threw her a five-dollar bill, then grabbed his backpack and car keys from the table, stuck his feet in his sneakers, and stormed out the door. Jumping into the BMW, Todd stepped on the gas and the engine roared to life. As he sped toward school, Jessica's laughter was still ringing in his head.

This isn't what I had in mind when I moved in,

Todd thought angrily. He wanted to cook breakfast for his girlfriend, not for her bratty sister! It was so typical. *Jessica can never just wish us well and leave us alone.*

Yes, that was it, Todd concluded a few minutes later as he pulled into the Sweet Valley High student parking lot. He and Elizabeth had run into a problem with this living-together experiment: a problem named Jessica. How could they feel romantic and focus on their relationship if Jessica was always underfoot? Two's company, three's a crowd. *But the day's young*, Todd thought, his spirits lifting. He still had all afternoon to make something special happen for him and Elizabeth.

"Todd is *what*?" Enid exclaimed as she and Elizabeth strolled down the hallway toward the cafeteria.

"Shh." Elizabeth put a finger to her lips. "I don't want the whole school to find out! You're the only person I'm telling."

Enid shook her curly reddish-brown hair, smiling. "Elizabeth Wakefield, you wild and crazy girl. Jessica's bad influence is finally rubbing off on you!"

"It's not wild and crazy at all," Elizabeth insisted. "In fact, Jess thinks we're totally boring. We're basically just . . . playing house." She smiled wryly.

Enid squeezed her arm. "It still sounds like fun."

"Yeah." Elizabeth shrugged. "I guess so."

"Well, either it is or it isn't!" Enid gave Elizabeth a bemused look. "I'm having a hard time reading you on this, Liz."

Elizabeth laughed. "That shows how well you know me. I'm having a hard time reading myself! I mean, last night was great. Todd made dinner, and we stayed up until all hours talking and, well, you know. It was the perfect date. But seeing him again when I woke up this morning, and knowing he'll be there when I get home from school this afternoon, it's just a bit much."

Reaching Enid's locker, they stepped out of the flow of traffic. Enid reached in and grabbed her lunch bag. "Aren't you worried your parents'll find out?" she asked.

Elizabeth considered. "Not really. The only way they'll find out is if Jessica tells, and she won't as long as Todd and I do all her chores for her. I'm not worried so much as . . ." She struggled to find the right word, then tried another tack. "How would you like it if Hugh moved in for a week?"

Enid's green eyes crinkled at the corners. "I'd love it! I never get to see enough of him, because he lives in a different town."

Elizabeth didn't say anything.

Enid shut her locker, and they continued down the hallway toward the lunchroom. "Just relax about it," she advised Elizabeth. "Have a good time with Todd. Remember why you're doing this: You love each other."

"You make it sound so easy," said Elizabeth.

"Cut loose a little. Enjoy yourself!" Enid reiterated. "Who knows when you'll have another opportunity like this!"

Entering the cafeteria, they met up with Penny Ayala and Olivia Davidson. "It's almost too hot to eat," Penny complained, tossing a plastic-wrapped tuna sandwich onto her tray.

Elizabeth chose the chef's salad. "I skipped breakfast because of that meeting, so I'm starving."

"You know what would hit the spot?" said Olivia. "A milk shake. An ice-cold strawberry milk shake."

"That settles it—we're going to the Dairi Burger after school!" Enid declared.

Elizabeth seconded the motion with enthusiasm. "I'm there. Let's meet outside after the—oh, hi, Todd."

"Hi, everybody," said Todd, slipping an arm around Elizabeth.

"Want to join us for lunch?" she offered.

Todd's arm tightened around her waist and he drew her aside. "Actually, I was hoping we could sit somewhere by ourselves," he murmured. "Just the two of us."

Elizabeth felt a momentary flash of annoyance. "I don't want to ditch my friends."

Todd dropped his voice to a whisper. "I want to talk about our plans for tonight, and we can't exactly do that with other people around, can we?"

Todd had a point. "All right." She gave Penny, Olivia, and Enid an apologetic smile. Enid winked

73

at her. "I need to talk to Todd about something," Elizabeth explained. "See you guys later."

Todd led the way to a corner table and Elizabeth followed him with her tray. "What's up?" she asked, taking his hand and giving it a squeeze. "How was breakfast with Jessica?"

"A complete disaster," Todd said cheerfully. "You'll have to get the details from her. How'd your meeting go?"

"Really well," replied Elizabeth, uncapping her bottle of lime-flavored seltzer water. "We ironed out the last-minute problems with the issue and even had time to stick in a story about the budget crunch at Project Youth. Penny had a total inspiration—to end the article with a challenge to students to come up with fund-raising projects to help save the program. Wasn't that a great idea?"

Todd, staring off into space, didn't answer. Elizabeth waved a hand in front of his face. "Hello, anybody home?"

"Sorry." Todd grinned sheepishly. "Guess I'm a little preoccupied."

"What's on your mind?"

"I was thinking about tonight," he replied, touching her foot with his under the table. "How about bribing Jessica to get out of the house so we could have a quiet, candlelit dinner, just the two of us?"

"That sounds nice," agreed Elizabeth, "but we have to do the laundry. It's Jessica's turn, and she's been letting it pile up for days."

74

Todd made a face, clearly dismayed by the prospect of trying to create a romantic atmosphere amid mountains of dirty laundry. Then he snapped his fingers. "I've got it. One of those laundry/video-rental/cappuccino bars just opened up in town. Why don't we try that?"

"But we can do laundry at home for free," Elizabeth pointed out.

"I know, but it could be fun," Todd pressed. He rubbed his foot along her ankle.

Going to the Laundromat sounds like fun? Has he lost his mind? Elizabeth wondered. But Todd was gazing at her with an appealing puppy-dog look. *I guess if he thinks it'll be romantic I should give it a try,* she decided. *I owe him that much, after ditching him yesterday afternoon and again this morning.*

"Okay, Todd," Elizabeth said with a smile. "If anyone can make a night at the Laundromat romantic, it's you. You're on."

"You're going *where*?" Jessica asked in disbelief late that afternoon.

"The Videomat," Elizabeth repeated, dropping a box of detergent on top of a highly piled laundry basket.

"That's a Laundromat, you know," Jessica informed her sister.

"No duh."

"Let me get this straight." Jessica leaned back against the washing machine, watching Elizabeth fill another big plastic basket with dirty clothes. "You and Todd just cooked dinner and cleaned the kitchen, and now you're going out for the night . . . to a Laundromat." She rolled her eyes. "Living with your boyfriend sure sounds exciting, Liz."

Elizabeth scowled at her twin. "We wouldn't have had to cook and clean and do laundry if you'd do your own chores!"

"A deal's a deal," Jessica said breezily. "Besides, you can't expect to get away with all play and no work."

"Why not? You manage to."

Jessica smiled complacently. "I do, don't I?"

"Well, don't wait up for us," Elizabeth said with a grunt, hoisting a laundry basket and stomping past Jessica. "We'll probably be late. There's about a hundred loads of laundry here!"

"I didn't realize so much had accumulated," Jessica lied. She waved after her sister. "Ta ta!"

As soon as Elizabeth, Todd, and the laundry took off in the Jeep, Jessica hitched herself up on the kitchen counter and grabbed the phone.

"The Videomat?" exclaimed Lila, sounding just as disgusted as Jessica. "That really is the saddest thing I've ever heard. Their parents are out of town, it's a once-in-a-lifetime opportunity to go crazy, and they do laundry."

"Can you believe I'm actually *related* to that girl?"

"Not really," Lila said. "Well, I have to see this."

"What, Todd and Liz at the Laundromat?"

76

"Todd and Liz at the Laundromat," Lila confirmed. "I'm totally blocked on this world-history assignment—I could use a study break."

"You're on. You call Pamela and I'll call Amy. Remember, though, no one can know Todd's staying over," Jessica added.

"My lips are sealed," Lila promised.

Chapter 7

"Mmm," Roger said. "Can I have more of that gazpacho? It really hit the spot."

Bruce clattered his spoon against the inside of his bowl. He'd finished his own soup, but really couldn't have said whether he'd liked it or not. Mrs. Patman ladled out some more soup for Roger, an artificially bright smile on her face. "Cold soup is so refreshing," she agreed. "I told Maria, 'No hot food tonight. We'll have cold soup, cold salmon, cold vegetables.'" She winked at the two boys. "The only thing hot will be the fudge on the sundaes!"

Bruce cracked a weak smile, but it took an effort. His mother's forced cheerfulness only made him more depressed. *Mom and Roger are trying so hard,* he thought. *How can they do it? How can they go on pretending that nothing's wrong?*

Bruce stared dully at the empty chair at the

head of the long dining-room table . . . his father's chair. An awkward silence fell over the room.

Roger obviously felt it was his duty to keep the conversation going. "It *is* hot," he observed unnecessarily. "Coach canceled track practice this afternoon because he didn't want people passing out from the heat. Kind of makes me wish I were on the swim team!"

Bruce didn't respond, and this time Mrs. Patman didn't, either. Once more they were enveloped in an anxious, oppressive silence.

Bruce shifted restlessly in his seat, wishing he could crawl out of his skin. He was in agony, imagining his father and Mrs. Wakefield together in Chicago, reliving their youthful romance. Tearing a piece of sourdough bread to bits, he darted a frantic glance at his mother. *Does Mom even know about Dad's other marriage?*

His curiosity was driving him crazy. *I have to ask her,* Bruce decided, *or I'll explode.* He opened his mouth to speak, but his mother beat him to it. "I—I have something to tell you boys," she began, her voice quavering. "I'm . . . I'm moving out tomorrow."

Bruce felt all the blood drain from his face. Roger's jaw dropped. "I'm renting a house on the other side of town, near the water, with plenty of room for both of you if you want to bring some of your things over," Mrs. Patman hurried to add. "Of course, this house will still be your home—I'd never ask you to leave it."

Her eyes searched her son's face, but Bruce remained stunned and speechless. "You boys will be OK here by yourselves for a few days, won't you?" she asked. "Maria will cook, and I'll be back and forth all week. I . . . just can't be here when Hank gets back from Chicago."

Suddenly her eyes filled with tears. She rose to her feet, putting a hand to her face to hide it from her son and nephew. "I should start packing. Excuse me."

Mrs. Patman hurried from the dining room, her heels clattering on the parquet floor. Bruce and Roger stared at each other. *A house on the other side of town?* Bruce thought, sick to his stomach. Although his parents had announced their decision to separate, this made it official.

Bruce realized that up until this moment, he'd been hoping against hope that his parents would reconcile. But with his mother moving out of the house . . .

Maria brought the salmon to the table, but Bruce knew he couldn't eat it. A wave of nausea washed over him, and he shoved back his chair. Without a word to Roger, he bolted from the room.

Upstairs, he rushed down the long hallway to his parents' suite. The door was open a crack; he peered in. Half a dozen suitcases were scattered about, and the king-size bed was piled with clothing. *She's leaving,* Bruce thought, his heart contracting with a knifelike pain. *She's really leaving.*

He shuffled back to his own room and sat on

the edge of his four-poster bed. Stretching out his arm, he picked up the phone from the bedside table. Without thinking, he punched in a number. It rang once, twice, three times. . . . An answering machine picked up. "You've reached the Wakefield family. No one can take your call right now, but if you leave your name . . ."

Bruce hung up quickly, his heart pounding. "What are you doing, Patman?" he asked himself out loud. He'd meant to dial Pamela's number.

Bruce stared at the phone, wondering. He needed to talk to someone, and he'd reached out. With no thought, with no premeditation, purely instinctively, he'd reached out . . . for Elizabeth Wakefield.

"How 'bout there?" Elizabeth said to Todd, gesturing with her laundry basket toward a table and some chairs. "No one seems to be using that TV and VCR."

Todd dumped his overloaded basket with a grunt. "I'll run out and get the rest of the laundry. Meet you in the video section."

Elizabeth wandered through the Videomat, checking out the scene. A little video shop was set up in one corner; across from that stretched a long counter where patrons sat chatting and sipping coffee. *This place is packed,* Elizabeth thought with amazement. *Todd was right—I guess it really is Sweet Valley's hottest new night spot!*

When Todd rejoined Elizabeth, he already had a movie in his hand. "Let's watch this," he suggested. "It's a classic—black and white."

Elizabeth read the title and wrinkled her nose in distaste. "Sorry, but I'm not in the mood for anything old and corny," she declared, thinking of last week's string of depressing matinees. "How about . . ." She scanned the shelves. ". . . this?"

Todd took the tape she'd selected. "A western?" he said. "You're kidding!"

"What's wrong with a western?" Elizabeth demanded. People turned to look, and Elizabeth lowered her voice. "We're doing laundry, for heaven's sake—do you want to be bored to tears? At least an action movie would liven things up!"

"Bored to tears?" Todd looked offended. "I thought we'd have fun as long as we were together. Maybe if we watched a romantic movie—"

Elizabeth frowned. "I just don't feel like watching a romance. Can't we compromise?"

"OK, OK." Todd tossed his movie back on the shelf and grabbed another at random. "Here's one I wouldn't mind seeing. Do you approve?"

Elizabeth shrugged. "It'll do."

They walked back to their table, stopping at the counter on the way to order two espressos. "Ugh, I can't drink this," Todd exclaimed after tasting the strong, dark coffee.

Elizabeth took an experimental sip. "Umm, I like it," she said, determined for some illogical reason to take the opposite stance from Todd on every issue. "I'll finish yours if you don't want it."

"I don't want it."

Todd stomped along the row of industrial-sized washing machines, flipping open the doors and throwing armfuls of dirty laundry into the machines. "Todd, you have to sort it!" Elizabeth protested. "Lights and darks go in separate loads. Do you want the dark stuff to bleed all over the whites?"

"No, of course not," Todd said through clenched teeth. "So sorry."

They sorted the laundry and then Todd shook powdered detergent into each machine while Elizabeth inserted the proper number of quarters. The machines started to fill with water; Todd collapsed in front of their TV while Elizabeth drained both cups of espresso. "I'm getting more coffee," she announced. Last night's lack of sleep was beginning to catch up with her, and she figured the caffeine might do her good. "Do you want anything?"

Todd shook his head, not even looking at her.

"What a grouch," Elizabeth complained to herself as she strolled to the coffee counter. "Why does he have to take everything so seriously?"

She paid for two more cups of espresso, one of which she finished on the way back to her seat. *The caffeine must be kicking in,* she thought, suddenly feeling energized. She bounced up to Todd, who had turned his back on the movie in order to peer anxiously through the glass door of one of the machines. "This one doesn't seem to be sudsing," he remarked.

"Add some more detergent," Elizabeth suggested. "Are you sure you don't want a cup of espresso?" She tickled his ribs. "It'll get your engines revving."

Todd jumped in surprise, dumping about half the box of detergent into the dispenser. "No, thanks, but maybe you shouldn't drink it, either—"

Elizabeth was already sipping the coffee. "*You* were the one who was all fired up to come here," she reminded him. "I'm just trying to make the best of it and have a good time. Lighten up!"

"I'll lighten up if you'll sit down with me and watch the movie," Todd bargained.

They tried it for a moment, but Elizabeth couldn't sit still. Hopping back to her feet, she started pacing in front of the machines. Suddenly she saw something that made a giggle rise in her throat. "Oh, To-odd," she sang, pointing. "Is that machine sudsing enough for you now?"

Todd turned in his chair to look. The machine that he'd added the extra detergent to had started to shake. The glass window on the front showed nothing but thick white suds pressing and swirling against the glass. An occasional jeans leg swiped desperately against the window, as though it were drowning. As they watched in fascination, bubbles began oozing out through the door. "Oh, no. It's going to blow!" Todd exclaimed.

As Todd moved over to the machine, Elizabeth saw somebody waving to her from across the room. Glancing over, she saw Jessica approaching with Lila, Amy, and Pamela in tow. "Hi, guys! Over here!" Elizabeth called cheerfully.

At that instant the washing-machine door sprang open and an ocean of white, foaming soap bubbles cascaded out onto the laundry-room floor. Todd stood there in disbelief, watching as sudsy foam swashed around his ankles and covered his sneakers. Elizabeth, Jessica, Lila, Pamela, and Amy all burst out laughing.

"It's not funny!" he snapped.

The sight of Todd wading through the bubbles in a desperate effort to unplug the machine only made Elizabeth laugh harder. "I'm sorry," she gasped, hiccuping. "It's just—"

She succumbed to another bout of giggles. Amy doubled over, slapping her thigh. Her eyes squeezed shut, Pamela laughed soundlessly. Lila and Jessica clung to each other, hooting at the tops of their lungs.

Up to his knees in bubbles, Todd put his hands on his hips and glared at Elizabeth. "What's so hysterical?"

"You really know how to show a girl a good time, Todd." Elizabeth wiped the tears of laughter from her eyes. "You were right about this evening. Laundry *can* be a lot of fun."

"I don't know if I'll ever be able to look at Todd

Wilkins the same way again," Pamela admitted, sipping her chocolate milk shake. After leaving the Videomat, Pamela, Jessica, Amy, and Lila had headed over to the Dairi Burger.

"He practically had to swim through the bubbles to get to the washing machine," Jessica recollected gleefully. "I really didn't expect such a great show!"

"We were in the right place at the right time," Lila agreed, crunching into an onion ring. "I make a habit of that, you know."

"Poor Liz." Pamela shook her head, her dark hair swinging. "I have a feeling there was a *big* fight coming."

Jessica waved a hand. "Don't feel sorry for them. One little squabble won't spoil their honeymoon."

Pamela saw Jessica wink at Lila. Lila rolled her eyes.

"By the way," said Amy, leaning forward with her elbows on the table. "Why were Todd and Liz doing laundry at the Videomat in the first place?"

Jessica and Lila exchanged another meaningful glance. "That's a very good question, Miss Sutton. Maybe I'll tell you one of these days, if you're nice to me," Jessica said with a sly grin.

Amy looked from Jessica to Lila and back again, her gray eyes sparkling with curiosity. "OK, guys, what's going on? Spill the beans!"

Pamela was about to make her own plea when she spotted a boy entering the restaurant. "Bruce!" she called eagerly.

Bruce strode toward their table. "Girls' night out?" he said in greeting.

"Yes. You forgot your dress, though," Jessica quipped.

Not responding to Jessica, Bruce pulled up a chair next to his girlfriend and turned his gaze on her. "I was hoping I'd find you here."

Pamela's lips curved in a pleased smile. "Yeah?"

"Yeah." Bruce took her hand, toying with the silver bracelet she wore on her wrist.

Pamela tried to read the expression in his eyes. Had something happened to upset him, or was he just in one of the quiet moods that had grown more common since his parents started having trouble? "Is anything . . . ? If you want, we can . . ." She squeezed his hand.

But Bruce shrugged off the private message she'd sent him, so she decided to leave it alone.

"We're glad you're here," Amy told Bruce. "We were just talking about guys who *seem* studly and cool but then turn out to be the opposite. Any insights you can share with us on that topic?"

"I don't know, Amy," Bruce countered. "After all, you know Barry better than I do."

Amy had to laugh, even though it was at her boyfriend, Barry Rourke's, expense.

Pamela smiled into her milk shake as Bruce, Lila, Amy, and Jessica entered into a spirited debate about the pros and cons of letting a guy do your laundry. Bruce was always telling her she was like a mother hen, worrying too much. *I have to remember that he's stronger than I give him credit for, stronger than I would be under the same circumstances,* Pamela thought. *He must be OK if he's making jokes, right?*

Todd rolled over on the sofa bed, pulling a pillow over his head to block out the morning sun. The sun . . .

Sitting bolt upright, he looked around wildly for the alarm clock. *It went off,* he remembered fuzzily, *and I picked it up and threw it across the room. . . .*

There was another clock on the far wall in the den. When Todd saw the time, he leaped off the sofa, tripping over a tangle of sheets. "Shoot, we're really going to be late for school!" He stumbled to the foot of the stairs. "Liz! Why'd you let me oversleep?" he shouted.

Still in her pajamas, Elizabeth appeared at the top of the stairs, rubbing her own bleary eyes. "What time is it?" she mumbled.

"Time to be leaving for school, that's what time it is," Todd told her. "Get in the shower and make it fast!"

Amazingly, they were ready to leave in only ten minutes. Dropping onto a chair in the kitchen, Todd pulled on his socks and sneakers while Elizabeth rummaged in the refrigerator for portable breakfast food. "I almost never sleep through my alarm," she remarked, sticking a couple of apples in her book bag. "I must've been really tired." She smiled brightly. "But I feel pretty good now!"

"Lucky you," Todd grumbled. "I don't do too well myself on only five hours of sleep. Do you know how late you kept me up, flipping TV channels and yapping your head off?"

Elizabeth laughed. "I was pretty wired, wasn't I?"

"Just promise me," Todd said wearily, "you won't ever drink four cups of espresso again."

"Six," she corrected him, grinning.

Shouldering his backpack, Todd opened the door for Elizabeth. She stepped outside and then checked her stride abruptly, clapping a hand over her mouth. "Ohmigod, the recycling!" she cried.

A feeling of doom percolated in Todd's empty stomach. "The recycling?" he repeated.

"We have to bundle the newspapers and separate the cans from the bottles. Usually Jessica does it," Elizabeth explained. "The recycling truck comes on Wednesdays—they'll be here any minute."

Doubling back to the garage, Elizabeth dumped a garbage bag full of recyclable materials on the floor and Todd started tossing them into the appropriate bins.

"I'll bring it to the curb," Todd said to Elizabeth. "Meet you at the car."

At that moment, the door opened and Jessica emerged, looking breezy and cool in a white cotton tank dress and ankle-wrap sandals. "How's married life?" she asked archly, sidestepping a pile of empty soda cans on her way to the Jeep. "Nice stunt last night at the Videomat, Todd." Todd glared after her, unable to come up with a suitable retort.

Dropping the bin by the curb after Jessica had backed the Jeep out of the driveway, he paused to mop the sweat from his forehead. As he did, a black Porsche pulled up. Todd didn't need to see the "1BRUCE1" license plate to recognize the car. *What's he doing here?* Todd wondered.

The driver's-side window buzzed down, and Todd could feel an air-conditioned breeze from the car's cool interior. "Hey, Wilkins," Bruce called, tapping on the horn. "Fancy meeting you here."

If Todd was surprised and annoyed to see Bruce, he was even more surprised when Elizabeth darted forward from the house, her book bag slung over her shoulder. Bending close to the car, she and Bruce exchanged a few quick words. Then Elizabeth turned to Todd. "Bruce is going to give me a ride to school," she announced, giving her boyfriend a perfunctory good-bye kiss. "He needs to talk to me about something really important. I'll see you later, OK?"

Before Todd could protest, Elizabeth had slipped into the passenger seat and the Porsche was roaring off down the street. Todd vented some of his frustration by kicking the recycling bin.

Chapter 8

"What's the matter?" Elizabeth asked Bruce as he gunned the engine and sped away from her house.

Bruce didn't answer immediately, and Elizabeth had a horrible suspicion he had evidence about her mother and Mr. Patman's affair.

"My mother's moving out," Bruce finally said as he sped through a yellow light. "She packed her bags last night."

Bruce's news wasn't as bad as she'd feared, but it was still very disturbing. Elizabeth's heart went out to him. "Oh, Bruce, I'm so sorry," she said, placing a hand on his arm.

Bruce's eyes were hidden behind dark sunglasses, but Elizabeth saw a tear roll down his cheek. He brushed it away quickly, clenching his jaw. "I'm really sorry," she repeated softly.

"Thanks," Bruce said, his voice scratchy. "I

don't know why, but I just felt like I needed to tell you. I hope it's OK that I barged over like that." He glanced at her, his mouth twisting in a smile. "I sure didn't think I'd catch Wilkins taking out your trash! What's the dirt, Wakefield?"

Elizabeth laughed, blushing. "Todd's staying over while our parents are out of town," she confessed. "But don't worry, Jessica's chaperoning us."

"Liz, I'm scandalized," Bruce teased. "Really, what will people say?"

"They won't say anything if you keep your mouth shut!" Elizabeth countered.

"Well . . ." Bruce hesitated. Elizabeth punched him lightly on the arm. "OK," he agreed. "Your secret's safe with me."

Shaking her head, Elizabeth smiled to herself. Who'd have thought she'd ever have a conversation like this with Bruce Patman?

When the laughing stopped, a strained, preoccupied silence fell over them. "I wish I knew what to say to make you feel better," Elizabeth said at last.

"You don't have to say anything," Bruce told her. "It helps just to be with someone who understands."

Someone who understands. *Why wasn't Bruce turning to Pamela at a time like this?* Elizabeth wondered. *Well, I'm just glad he feels he can trust me. That's what friends are for, right?*

As they got closer to school, Elizabeth found herself growing tense and troubled. While it was nice Bruce considered her someone he could turn to, she was starting to wish he hadn't confided in her. His mother moving out was a pretty big deal.

The more Elizabeth thought about this, the more worried she became. Did that mean her mom was that much closer to moving in?

The bell signaling the start of lunch period rang, and Elizabeth joined the throng of students flowing toward the cafeteria. Then she halted abruptly and did an about-face.

I just can't deal with it today, Elizabeth decided, heading away from the cafeteria. *I can't deal with . . .*

"Hey, Liz, wait up!"

Elizabeth stopped again so Enid could catch up with her. "Hi. I didn't see you."

"That's because you were moving too fast," said Enid, falling into step alongside her friend. "Who are you running away from?"

Elizabeth raised her eyebrows. "Was I running?"

Enid laughed. "Sprinting's more like it! Do you have a meeting or something?"

Elizabeth shook her head. "I just decided to spend lunch period at the *Oracle* office," she explained. "Besides, I—"

"What?" Enid prompted.

"This is going to sound terrible," Elizabeth warned, "but I'm kind of . . . avoiding Todd."

Enid blinked, surprised. "How come? Aren't you two having fun . . ." She lowered her voice. "You know, living together?"

"Let's just say we're having our ups and downs." Elizabeth described the previous night's laundromat misadventure. "I don't know." She frowned, frustrated at her inability to give a name to her restless feelings. "Maybe I'm not getting enough time to myself. I haven't been able to write in my journal, or hang out with you or anybody else besides Todd. I feel cut off."

"So tell Todd you need some time to yourself—an hour a night. He'll understand."

"I'm not so sure. He's being pretty possessive." They reached the door to the *Oracle* office. "I've also been thinking a lot about my mom, and I can't seem to do both at once. Think about my mom and about Todd, I mean."

Enid gave Elizabeth's arm a supportive squeeze. "I'll leave you alone to get some work done. Call me later, though, OK?"

"I will," Elizabeth promised.

As Enid headed back toward the cafeteria, Elizabeth ducked into the empty newspaper office.

Settling down at a desk in the corner, she pulled out her sandwich and the small spiral notebook she was using to take notes for the biography of her mother. Now that half the day had gone by, she wasn't quite as upset about what Bruce had revealed on the way to school. But she was still very confused about the whole situation. She needed to sort the fact from the conjecture. *I'll make two categories,* she decided. *What I know, and what I just think I know.* The process of writing would help her straighten out her thoughts; it always did.

Scribbling in her notebook, Elizabeth wasn't aware of the time passing until the office door swung open and Mr. Collins, the *Oracle's* adviser and Elizabeth's favorite English teacher, walked in.

"I didn't expect to find you here!" Mr. Collins greeted Elizabeth. "Todd's been looking for you."

Elizabeth shrugged. "Is lunch over already?"

"Not yet. I was looking for a quiet place to grade some papers," Mr. Collins said. "Mind if I pull up a chair?"

"Go right ahead," Elizabeth replied.

For a few minutes Elizabeth and Mr. Collins worked in companionable silence. Then he laughed out loud. "I'm sorry," he said, his blue eyes crinkling at the corners. "But some of the bloopers in these freshman papers are just too funny."

Elizabeth smiled. "I'm sure I committed some good ones myself."

"No, you're a born writer, Elizabeth."

"These days I'm not so sure." She tapped her pencil on her notebook. "This biography assignment is turning out to be harder than I expected."

"Well, I had hoped it would be challenging," Mr. Collins acknowledged.

Challenging—what an understatement! Still tapping the pencil, Elizabeth thought hard. She often turned to Mr. Collins for advice about personal matters as well as academic ones, and he was always unfailingly supportive, encouraging, and honest. She couldn't ask him outright, though; she'd have to pose a hypothetical question.

"Mr. Collins . . ."

He looked up at her, his eyebrows lifted inquiringly.

"How would you react," Elizabeth began, "if you found out something about someone you thought you knew better than anyone in the world—something shocking, something you can't believe is true . . . but it is?"

"Hmm . . ." Mr. Collins considered, his forehead wrinkled. "I imagine I'd probably start to question everything I thought I knew about him or her."

Elizabeth nodded slowly. *That's exactly what's happening to me,* she realized. No matter how hard she tried to deny it, no matter how many times she reorganized her notes, the evidence continued to point to the likelihood that her mother was having an affair. *It doesn't fit with my opinion of Mom's character, but since I found out she was married to someone else before Dad . . . anything's possible—anything at all!*

When the final bell rang on Wednesday, Todd made a beeline for Elizabeth's locker. He'd been looking for her all day, but he always seemed to just miss her. *She has to show up here, though,* he thought, leaning back against the locker. *She knows I always stop by to see her before basketball practice.*

The crowd swirled around him; the corridor echoed with voices and laughter and the sound of locker doors slamming. Gradually the crowd thinned as students dispersed to after-school sports and activities or headed for home. Still no Elizabeth. *How could I have missed her?* Todd wondered.

He strode to the *Oracle* office. The door was ajar, and he smiled as he pushed it open, expecting to see Elizabeth. Instead he found Tina Ayala and Allen Walters sorting through a pile of black-and-white photos. "Have you seen Elizabeth?" Todd asked.

Tina and Allen shook their heads.

"Well, if she shows up, tell her I stopped by, OK? Thanks."

Todd headed next to the school library, where he checked every carrel and study table to no avail. Finally heading toward the gym, he stopped at a pay phone in the lobby and stuck in a coin, dialing Elizabeth's number on the off chance that she'd headed straight home. The machine answered; Todd hung up with a discouraged sigh.

As he shuffled toward the locker room, a puzzled frown creased his forehead. He couldn't help wondering if she was avoiding him and why this living together thing wasn't working better. *Why aren't we having fun?* Todd asked himself.

Dumping his sports bag on the bench in front of his gym locker, Todd stripped off his khaki pants and polo shirt and rummaged around for a clean T-shirt. As he sat down to pull on a pair of crew socks, Winston and Bill materialized, with wet hair and towels draped around their necks.

Bill snapped his towel at Todd. "Hey, Wilkins," he said cheerfully. "How's it going?"

Todd couldn't lie. "Not so hot," he admitted.

Winston dropped down on the bench next to Todd and peered into his face with a penetrating expression. "Let me guess. Girl trouble?"

"How'd you know?" Todd exclaimed.

Winston shrugged, grinning. "What else is there?"

Bill wrinkled his sun-freckled nose. "You and Liz aren't . . ."

"We're not breaking up or anything," Todd said. "We're just . . ." What? "Actually, we're . . ." He lowered his voice. "Can I trust you guys to keep a secret?"

"Sure," Winston declared.

"You bet," confirmed Bill.

"My folks are out of town this week, and so are hers, so I'm staying over at her house," Todd confided.

Winston elbowed him, grinning. "You devil!"

Bill whistled his approval. "Who would have thought? Our little Todd, so—"

"It's not as hot as it sounds," Todd interrupted. "Jessica's sticking us with all her chores and making me cook breakfast for her just so she won't broadcast it. And every five minutes Elizabeth runs off to hold Patman's hand because for some reason

98

he's decided to dump all his problems on her. And last night at the Videomat . . ."

Todd told the story. Winston guffawed. "Man, I would've loved to see that!"

"You would've played it up for all it was worth. I just lost my temper and looked like a jerk."

"So, make it up to her," Bill said simply. "Do something nice for her."

"Like what?" asked Todd.

"Treat her like a princess," Winston recommended in a sage, world-wise tone. He puffed out his narrow chest. "Flowers, presents, a candlelit dinner—the works! Take my word for it, girls love that stuff. Maria does, anyway," he added.

"Egbert's right. For once," Bill said. "You need to let Liz know that you don't take her for granted. You still think being with her is incredibly special."

"Hmm." Todd considered his friends' advice. *Maybe it wasn't fair to get mad when she went off with Bruce this morning,* he reflected. *I've got to try harder to understand what she's going through.*

"You know, you guys may have something there," Todd said thoughtfully.

Bill slapped him on the shoulder. "Shower her with love and attention."

"She'll be putty in your hands," Winston declared heartily.

Elizabeth sat under a tree on the lawn behind the high school, her spiral notebook open on her

99

lap. The breeze that ruffled her hair was as hot and dry as an oven; it had to be ninety-five degrees even in the shade.

Tipping her head back against the tree trunk, Elizabeth closed her eyes and fantasized about diving into the cool water of the swimming pool in her backyard. *If I left now, I could be in my bathing suit in ten minutes.*

Elizabeth glanced at her watch and sighed. It was nearly four. She'd been blowing Todd off all day. *I really should hang around so at least we can drive home together.* Elizabeth closed her eyes again, fanning herself with the notebook. Her eyelids drooped, then closed. . . .

An hour and a half later, Elizabeth's eyes popped open and she sat up like a jack-in-the-box. Blinking sleepily, she brushed the blades of grass from her bare arms.

Gathering up her things, Elizabeth scrambled to her feet and set off for the gym. The gym was empty, so she ran to the parking lot . . . just in time to see Todd's black BMW exit the lot and speed off.

Elizabeth waved her arms, even though there was no chance of flagging Todd down. *Rats. Well, maybe Jessica's still here,* she thought. A quick scan of the parking lot, however, revealed that the Jeep, too, was gone.

At that moment she noticed someone signaling to her from the other side of the parking lot. Elizabeth narrowed her eyes against the blinding afternoon sun. Elizabeth waved back. "Hi, Bruce!"

"Need a ride?" he called.

Thinking about Todd's expression as she drove off with Bruce that morning, Elizabeth hesitated, but only for a second. "Actually, I do," she called back. "If it's not too much trouble."

"Kind of hot for tennis-team practice," Elizabeth remarked as Bruce pointed the Porsche in the direction of Calico Drive.

"It was brutal," Bruce agreed.

"I can't wait to get into the pool." Elizabeth lifted the hair off the back of her neck. "I may not get out again until this heat wave is over!"

Bruce managed to crack a smile.

"Will you go for a swim when you get home?" she asked conversationally.

Bruce shrugged. "I don't know if I am going home," he mumbled, flicking on his turn signal. "I might take a drive. I just don't think I can stand to be there, with my mom gone and all."

Elizabeth turned to Bruce impulsively. "Look, why don't you come over for a while?" she suggested. "We could take a swim, have something to eat."

Bruce glanced at her, his eyebrows cocked. "Wilkins won't mind?"

"It's *my* house," Elizabeth reasoned.

"Looks like no one's home," Bruce observed, glancing around.

They'd pulled the Porsche into the garage to

get it out of the sun. "Yeah, no Jeep and no BMW," Elizabeth said, leading the way into the kitchen. "I wonder where everybody is."

She took out a pitcher of lemonade and poured two glasses. They drank in silence, looking at each other out of the corners of their eyes. *This is a little weird*, Bruce thought. He felt as though they needed a reason to hang around together. "I've been thinking about what happened the other day in my attic."

A very faint blush tinted Elizabeth's cheeks. "You have?"

Bruce peered at Elizabeth, a smile curving his lips. "You're blushing!"

"I am not!" she protested, grabbing a magazine from the stack of mail lying on the table in order to fan herself. "I'm roasting, that's all."

Bruce shrugged, still smiling. "Well, anyway, I was wondering if you found everything there was to find in *your* attic."

"I was pretty thorough," Elizabeth said, "but you never know." She wrinkled her nose. "There's so much clutter up there, and it's so darned hot. . . ." She smiled. "But what the heck. It's worth another look!"

On the second floor, Elizabeth pulled the fold-out ladder from the ceiling and they climbed up into the smotheringly hot attic. "The photo was in here," Elizabeth said, raising the lid of a dusty trunk, "along with this."

Gently Elizabeth lifted an armful of tissue

paper from the trunk. She unwrapped the paper, revealing a long white wedding gown.

"Wow," Bruce breathed. "It's the dress your mom's wearing in the picture!"

Elizabeth nodded. "And here are the shoes, and the flowers."

Bruce gaped at the souvenirs, carefully hidden away in the trunk for all these years. Putting out a hand, he touched the dress. It was very real, very tangible; he could almost see Alice Wakefield wearing it . . . with his own father standing next to her in his wedding attire.

Elizabeth replaced the dress. "There's really nothing else up here," she said.

"What's this?" Bruce pulled a couple of pieces of old, yellowed newspaper out of the trunk.

"Oh, it's just in there for stuffing."

Bruce examined the newspaper. "Hey, it's their college paper!" he said.

Elizabeth's eyes read over Bruce's shoulder. "Look at the date—it's from when our parents were in college."

"I bet it's from close to the time of the wedding," Bruce guessed. "That would've been when your mother packed the dress away."

"Look at these headlines," Elizabeth said, snatching the paper out of Bruce's hands. "What a crazy time—peace rallies, rock concerts . . ."

"'Make love, not war,' right?"

"Check this out," Elizabeth said, hoping he

wouldn't notice that she was blushing again. "It's about a big student sit-in at the administration building. According to this, the students were able to hold out so long because someone airdropped food to the roof of the building from a helicopter!"

"What a stunt," Bruce said admiringly.

Elizabeth took a closer look at the picture accompanying the story. Her eyes widened. "You're not going to believe this."

"Believe what?" Bruce asked.

Elizabeth read aloud, "'Manna From Heaven: Hank Patman Orchestrates Helicopter—'"

Bruce gasped in disbelief. "What the . . . ? Hank Patman? Dad did *that*?"

Elizabeth showed him the photo of students holding out their hands for the bundles of food. "I'd bet anything my mom was part of the sit-in," she said, excited. "She was into that kind of thing."

"Yeah, but my father? A tie-dyed hippie radical?" Bruce shook his head, flabbergasted. "It's inconceivable. His politics have always been to the right of right. I mean, conservativism runs in the family."

"Maybe it didn't always." Elizabeth tipped her head thoughtfully. "It *was* the sixties. Maybe something like that sit-in was what drew our folks together. Of course!" She put a hand on Bruce's arm. "This must have been the 'heroic' thing my mom referred to in her letter!"

Bruce stared into Elizabeth's eyes. Electricity crackled between them. "You know what we have to do now," he said, his voice intense.

Elizabeth held her breath.

"We have to go there. To the college. We have to find out more about the sit-in and the airdrop. We have to find out who my dad was, who your mom was, all those years ago. Maybe then we'll understand what's motivating them now."

"Tomorrow," Elizabeth agreed. "After school."

Chapter 9

Using the spare key Elizabeth had loaned him, Todd unlocked the front door and pushed it open with his knee. In one hand he gripped a bouquet of roses and a gift-wrapped jewelry box. The other arm clutched two bulging grocery bags.

"Honey, I'm home," he yelled as he stepped into the hall. From the kitchen, he heard the murmur of voices. *Liz and Jess,* Todd guessed as he headed in that direction. *Well, needless to say, I'd rather get Elizabeth alone, but I won't let Jessica spoil my surprise.* "Elizabeth, *ma petite fleur,*" he called cheerfully in a ridiculous French accent, "tonight for zee dinner, I am going to prepare for you zee *specialité de la maison—*"

He reached the doorway to the kitchen and halted, the grocery bags nearly slipping from his arms. Elizabeth and Bruce, wearing swimsuits, were sitting at the kitchen table, a pitcher of iced tea and a plate of cookies between them.

I'm dreaming, Todd thought grimly.

"Hey, Wilkins," Bruce greeted him with a broad grin. "What's for dinner?"

The grocery bags slipped another notch. Todd stared at Bruce, and then at Elizabeth. She smiled weakly. "Hi, Todd."

Todd turned and dumped the groceries, the roses, and the jewelry box on the counter. "Fancy meeting you here, Bruce," he said with barely veiled sarcasm.

Bruce sat back in his chair, folding his arms behind his head. "Yeah, well, Elizabeth told me to pull my car into the garage to keep it out of the sun."

"Hope it's OK that I invited Bruce to stay for dinner," Elizabeth said, her tone placating. "If we don't have enough food, I can run out and—"

"There's plenty of food," Todd grumbled. "I'll just make it for three instead of two."

"Four," Elizabeth corrected him. "Don't forget Jessica."

"Right. How could I forget Jessica?"

Getting to her feet, Elizabeth joined Todd at the counter. "The roses are beautiful," she said, looking up at him with a smile. "Are they for me?"

Todd smiled crookedly. "No, they're for Patman."

"Todd, you shouldn't have!" Bruce declared, putting a hand to his cheek in a coy gesture.

"He knows, by the way," Elizabeth whispered in

Todd's ear as she helped him unload the groceries. "About us. This week."

"Great," Todd whispered back. "That's just dandy."

Changing the subject, she said, "You know, you don't have to do all the cooking yourself. We'd be happy to pitch in."

"Don't worry about it," Todd replied stiffly. He nudged the jewelry box out of sight behind the toaster. He wasn't about to present a gift to Elizabeth with Bruce for an audience.

Elizabeth shrugged. "All right, if that's the way you want it."

"Why don't we get out of Todd's hair," Bruce suggested to her, gathering up the drinks. "We could take this stuff outside."

"We'll be on the patio," Elizabeth said to Todd. "Let us know when you're ready and we'll fire up the grill."

Todd watched Elizabeth and Bruce head out to the patio and make themselves comfortable on a couple of lounge chairs. *So much for Bill and Winston's advice,* he thought angrily. *Putty in my hands. Yeah, right.*

"Yum, something smells delicious," Jessica declared as she strolled into the kitchen half an hour later. "Lila and I spent the afternoon shopping at the mall—I'm ravenous." Jessica hitched herself up onto a stool. "By the way, is that Bruce's car in the garage?"

"Do you know anyone else who drives a black Porsche with the license plate '1BRUCE1'?" Todd asked.

Jessica raised her eyebrows. She reached for the fruit bowl and popped a grape in her mouth. "Hmm." She looked at Todd sweating over a hot stove, and then she glanced out to the backyard, where her sister and Bruce appeared to be enjoying the late afternoon. It didn't take a detective to figure out that Todd had been burned—again.

Poor Todd, Jessica thought, repressing a smile. *I really should try to rub salt in his wounds—I mean, soothe his injured feelings! That's what I meant. Of course.* "Liz and Bruce sure are spending a lot of time together," she observed innocently.

Todd got some vegetables out of the refrigerator and started chopping furiously.

"I mean, considering the fact that you're staying over this week," Jessica continued. "I thought you two would be inseparable."

Todd whacked a red pepper in half with the cleaver.

"I guess what makes it really interesting is that Liz always despised Bruce, but now suddenly he's all she talks about." This wasn't true, but Jessica enjoyed the look of shock and dismay on Todd's face when she said it. "Bruce, Bruce, Bruce. It's such a bore!"

Todd threw the diced red pepper into a bowl and seized a head of broccoli. "Liz is just . . ." Todd gave the broccoli a vigorous chop. ". . . Friendly. That's all."

109

"She certainly is." Grabbing the bunch of grapes, Jessica waltzed toward the sliding glass door to the patio, smiling slyly. "Lucky for you you're not the jealous type!"

Outside, Jessica greeted Bruce and Elizabeth, then wandered into the side yard with the portable telephone. "Drop everything, Li, and drive over *now*," Jessica hissed when her friend answered the phone.

"Why?" asked Lila in a small, tight voice.

"What's the matter? You sound strange," Jessica told her.

"I just put on some of that new cucumber and clay face mask we bought at the mall," Lila explained, her words clipped. "My facial muscles are sort of immobilized."

"Well, wash it off and get over here," Jessica insisted. "It looks like Mr. and Mrs. Todd Wilkins are about to perform for us again."

"Better than the Videomat?"

"Ten times better," Jessica promised. "*And* you'll get a gourmet dinner, too."

"I'll be there in ten minutes."

Back in the kitchen, Jessica leaned back against the counter and gave Todd a big smile. "I was just talking to Lila," she said, "and on the spur of the moment, I invited her over for dinner. I didn't think you'd mind, since Liz already invited Bruce." She pointed at the big glass bowl where chunks of beef were marinating for shish kebab. "It looks like there's plenty of food."

Todd slammed a bag of carrots down on the counter. "This isn't a restaurant, you know," he barked. "And what about being discreet? I thought we made a deal."

"I'm being very discreet," Jessica protested. "Just because Lila's coming over to see you cook dinner doesn't mean she—"

"To see me cook dinner, eh?" Todd interrupted.

Oops, Jessica thought.

Todd smiled mirthlessly. "Lila won't figure it out because you already told her, didn't you?"

"Look," said Jessica, her hands on her hips. "The point is, you have to do things my way, remember? As long as you do, I won't tell and Lila won't tell. But if you don't . . ."

Todd heaved a defeated sigh. "Fine. I'll be delighted to wait on you *both* hand and foot."

"You're a prince, Todd." Jessica reached over to pat his cheek in a condescending, grandmotherly fashion. "Liz is one lucky—" She broke off, spotting a small, glittering package peeking out from behind the toaster. "Ooh, a present!" she squealed. "Todd, is it for me?"

Todd shrugged resignedly. "Why not?"

Jessica ripped off the paper eagerly and opened the box. "Earrings! They're beautiful!" She held the dangly silver and turquoise earrings up to her face. "You shouldn't have, Todd."

He sighed again. "I know."

"Thanks a mil." Slipping the earrings on, Jessica

111

gave her head a little shake to make them dance. "You know, Todd, this is really turning out to be a great week. In my opinion, you can live with Liz anytime you want!"

"Excellent shish kebab," Bruce said. "Can I get your marinade recipe, Todd?"

Lila laughed; Todd glowered.

"It must be a Wilkins family secret," Elizabeth joked when her boyfriend didn't reply. "Something more to drink, Bruce?"

"No, thanks. I could go for seconds of the pasta salad, though."

"Here you go." Elizabeth passed the bowl his way. Then she smiled at Jessica. "This is fun. Kind of like a dinner party! I'm glad you could stay, Bruce. You, too, Lila."

Bruce grinned. "Anytime."

Todd had remained stubbornly silent throughout dinner. *What a wet blanket,* Elizabeth thought. *He'd probably pictured a candlelit dinner for two, but that's just too bad.* It was fun to have company for a change, instead of being so secretive. Besides, she rationalized, she couldn't have made Bruce go home and eat all by himself at the mansion.

"I'm sorry we weren't more organized," Elizabeth said out loud. "We could have called Pamela and invited her over too."

Bruce shrugged. "She's probably tied up over at Project Youth."

112

"I bet she's pretty bummed about what's happening there, huh?" said Jessica, sipping her iced tea.

"A lot of people are bummed," Lila commented. Lila had gone to Project Youth for counseling herself.

"That reminds me," Bruce said. "I had a great fund-raising idea when we were prowling around in the attic before, Liz."

"Prowling around in the attic?" Todd asked.

Elizabeth focused on Bruce. "What kind of idea?"

"We could have an auction. We'd get people to donate big things, like furniture—good, quality stuff."

"There were some real treasures in your attic," Elizabeth recalled, catching some of Bruce's enthusiasm. "People would pay real money for stuff like that."

"Bruce's attic?" Todd asked, but no one paid attention to him.

"And it would all go to Project Youth." Bruce's bright blue eyes flashed triumphantly. "What do you guys think?"

Todd just grunted. Jessica yawned. "Not bad," said Lila.

"Well, I think it's a great idea," Elizabeth declared. "I'm really . . ." *I'm really impressed,* she'd almost said. This was an altruistic, civic-minded side of Bruce Elizabeth hadn't seen before—she wouldn't have believed it even existed.

"Of course, I'd organize the whole thing." Bruce flashed an ultra-bright smile. "We could probably hold the auction at my house. Plenty of space."

"Maybe this won't be the end for Project Youth after all," Lila said.

"It's the old volunteer spirit," said Bruce modestly. "It can make all the difference."

Oblivious to Jessica and Lila, who were rolling their eyes, Elizabeth gazed raptly at Bruce across the dinner table. As he looked back at her, a half-smile on his face, she sensed a current of energy running between them. *We're on the same wavelength,* Elizabeth marveled. *Me and Bruce Patman!*

Elizabeth darted a glance at her sulky, antisocial boyfriend. She and Todd might as well have been living on different planets.

"Sure you can't stay?" Todd heard Jessica ask Lila after dinner.

"I hate to eat and run, but I have to get home and make some phone calls," Lila replied.

The two girls put their heads together; whispers and giggles drifted in Todd's direction. "Don't tell *too* many people," he thought he heard Jessica whisper.

Todd clattered a few dishes in the sink to drown out Lila's and Jessica's voices. He couldn't drown out Bruce's, though.

"That homemade strawberry shortcake was awesome," Bruce said as he helped Elizabeth clear the table. "Todd, I had no idea you were so handy in the kitchen!"

Todd gritted his teeth. "Well, see you tomorrow in school, Bruce."

It was a pretty blatant hint, but Todd didn't care about being tactful. *I've had about as much of Patman as I can take,* he thought, ignoring Elizabeth's glare.

"In here, Bruce!" Jessica called from the family room. Bruce put his hands in his pockets, smiled sheepishly at Todd, and sauntered off to the family room.

Elizabeth turned away, about to follow Bruce. "Hold on, Liz. Can I talk to you for a minute?" Todd requested. He was trying to hold on to his self-control, but the innocent, inquiring look on Elizabeth's face pushed him over the edge. "What is he *doing* here?" he exploded as soon as Bruce was out of earshot.

"I invited him to stay for dinner because he's upset about his mom moving out of the house."

Todd snapped a dish towel at the counter. "Well, how long does he have to stick around?" he asked peevishly.

"Look, this isn't your house." Elizabeth placed her hands on her hips, her eyes glittering angrily. "I can invite whomever I choose!"

"Of course," Todd said stiffly. "Sorry to be so *presumptuous*."

Facing the sink, he turned on the hot water and squirted some dishwashing liquid onto a dirty skillet. He felt Elizabeth's hand on his arm. "I didn't mean for it to come out that way," she said, her voice softer. "I just want Bruce to know he has my sympathy, that's all."

"Well, what about *me*?" Todd knew he sounded petty and childish, but he couldn't help it.

Elizabeth drew back. "What about you?" She shook her head in disbelief. "How can you be so selfish, Todd? You got stuck cooking—sorry, but so what? Think about what *he's* going through!" Turning on her heel, she flounced from the kitchen, the door banging shut behind her.

Todd washed the pots and pans and loaded up the dishwasher, but his blood pressure was still soaring when he stalked into the family room ten minutes later to join the others.

What he saw didn't improve his mood. Bruce was slumped comfortably on the sofa, a Wakefield twin sitting on either side of him, the remote control in his hand. Todd glared at him. Bruce just smiled up at him benevolently.

"I can't get over that ending," Jessica sniffled as the credits came up on the screen. "I really thought they were going to live happily ever after."

"That's life, baby," Bruce said bitterly, flipping channels with the remote control.

"Whoa, stop there!" Jessica instructed Bruce. "*Video Jukebox*—let's watch it."

Out of the corner of her eye, Jessica saw Todd shift impatiently in his chair.

"I hate this song," Bruce announced as a new video began. "I can't believe someone actually called in and requested it."

"Let's call in one we like," Jessica suggested. "How about Jamie Peters, 'Lawless Love'?"

Bruce stood up to get the telephone. Shoving the box of tissues aside, his eyes fell on a message scrawled on a notepad. "Hey, room four forty-four. That's my dad's room at the Drake Hotel in Chicago," he remarked.

"No," Jessica said, "it's my mom's room at the Drake Hotel in Chicago."

Suddenly Jessica realized what she'd just said— and so did Bruce, Elizabeth, and Todd. All four were silent as the shocking truth sank in. *Oh, no,* Jessica thought, *Mom and Mr. Patman are sharing a hotel room! Liz was right—they are having an affair!*

Bruce had frozen in the act of reaching for the phone. When it rang right under his hand, he jumped as if he'd been shot. Picking up the receiver, he handed it wordlessly to Jessica.

"H—Hello?" Jessica stuttered.

"Jessica? It's Dad. Sorry to call so late—did I wake you?"

Dad! Jessica's throat went dry. "No, Dad, we're still up," she replied, glancing in panic at Elizabeth. "How's it going?"

"It's going well. They're keeping us pretty busy, though, which is why I didn't phone you until now. How about you? Everything OK at home?"

"Everything's . . . fine," Jessica managed. "There's absolutely no news—nothing's happening at all," she hurried to add, before her father could get suspicious.

117

Mr. Wakefield laughed. "Well, I just wanted to say hi. Have you heard from your mother?"

Jessica gulped. "Have we heard from Mom?" She exchanged a desperate look with Elizabeth. "Um, yeah. She left a message a couple days ago. Why?"

"I just wondered if she'd had time to check in with you. I know she's busy too."

Yeah, busy having an affair with Mr. Patman. Jessica felt sick to her stomach. "Well, thanks for calling, Dad," she choked out. "We'll see you on Sunday."

"Bye, hon."

Jessica hung up the phone and got to her feet. Bruce was already on his way to the door, Elizabeth right behind him. "Good night," Bruce said, his somber eyes fixed on Elizabeth's face.

"Good night," Elizabeth whispered.

The door closed behind Bruce, and the house fell silent. Suddenly a strangled sob tore from Elizabeth's throat. Clasping a hand to her mouth, she ran up the stairs. Jessica dashed after her, leaving Todd alone in the hallway.

Upstairs, Jessica followed Elizabeth into her room. "What are we going to do, Liz?" Jessica exclaimed, clutching her sister's arm. "Should we call Dad back and tell him?" She imagined her father's reaction. *It would be just like a scene in a movie!* Jessica thought. *He'd hop on the next plane to Chicago. He'd burst into room four forty-four at the Drake—he'd probably shoot Mr. Patman!*

"No, Jessica, we're not going to tell Dad. Mom

will do the telling . . . if there's anything to tell."

"*If* there's anything to tell?" Jessica snorted. "They're sharing a hotel room, Liz. I think that's news."

All at once Elizabeth's face lit up with a fragile hope. "Maybe Bruce made a mistake," she said. "Maybe one of us got the room number wrong. I bet Mr. Patman's room is next to Mom's, or down the hall or something."

"Well, there's one way to find out." Jessica picked up the phone on Elizabeth's bedside table and dialed the number for the Drake. "We'll call the hotel and ask. It's as simple as that."

Elizabeth grabbed the receiver from Jessica's hand and slammed it down. "We can't do that," she whispered. "We just can't."

For a long minute, the two sisters sat in heavy silence, pondering the fact that their family might be about to fall to pieces. *What if Mom marries Mr. Patman?* Jessica thought in despair. As if one Wakefield/Patman romance wasn't distasteful enough . . .

Jessica swung around, pointing a finger at Elizabeth. "And while we're at it, what about *you*?" she demanded. "What's going on with you and Bruce?"

Elizabeth stared at Jessica, her cheeks flaming a hot pink. "Not a thing. What are you talking about?"

Jessica had caught her sister off guard, and her feelings were written all over her face.

Mom and Mr. Patman, Liz and Bruce . . . What's the world coming to?

119

Chapter 10

"Hey, big guy!" Winston caught up with Todd in the hall on the way to homeroom on Thursday morning and slapped him on the shoulder. "How'd it go with Liz last night? Did you rekindle the fickle flames of romance?"

"You don't want to know."

"But I do," Winston persisted jovially. "As your personal adviser on the subject of women, as Sweet Valley High's resident expert, I might add, I have a professional interest. Spill the beans!"

"OK. I bought a nice present . . . which I ended up giving to Jessica. And I cooked an elaborate meal . . . for Lila Fowler and Bruce Patman. The whole thing backfired!"

Winston frowned, scratching his head. "Wow. This almost never happens. Well, if Plan A doesn't work, I say forge ahead with Plan B. Why don't you—"

Stop taking advice from clowns like Egbert!
Todd thought bitterly. "Thanks, but no thanks," he
interrupted. "I think I can handle it on my own."

"Are you sure? Because I was going to suggest
my tried-and-true, patented formula for sweeping
a girl off her—"

"Gotta run!" Todd broke into a jog. "Catch you
later!"

Bruce grabbed a desk in the back row of homeroom so he could tip his chair against the wall and
snooze. When he'd gotten home from the Wakefields' the night before, he'd found a bunch of
messages on the answering machine from his
mother, urging him to come spend the night at her
new place if he was lonely. Peeking into Roger's
room, Bruce had seen that his cousin was already
sound asleep. Bruce had scornfully dismissed his
mother's invitation. *Does she think I'll be afraid of
the dark just because my mommy's not home?*

Maybe he hadn't been lonely or afraid, but
something had given him insomnia. He'd tossed
and turned all night, finally dozing off at sunrise.

The sound of his own name on the loudspeaker
caused Bruce to snap wide awake. "The newspaper
staff and Project Youth volunteers will co-sponsor a
lunch-period meeting to start organizing fund-raising projects for the Youth Center," Principal
Cooper announced. "Penny Ayala informs us that a
couple of great suggestions came in just this morn-

121

ing, including Bruce Patman's idea for a 'Clean-Out-Your-Attic Auction.' Come to the meeting if you'd like to get involved."

Bruce brought his chair back down on all four legs with a bang, acknowledging his classmates' curious, admiring glances with a disinterested shrug. When the bell finally rang, he bolted for the door, wanting to avoid having to make conversation.

Pamela intercepted him halfway to his locker. "Bruce!" she exclaimed, her eyes sparkling like sapphires. "I'm so excited about the fund-raising auction!" She linked her arm through his, pressing close to his side as they strolled down the hall. "I can't believe you kept such a great idea secret from me."

"Not a secret, really," Bruce said. "It was only last night that it just kind of occurred to me."

Pamela squeezed his arm. "I'm really touched that you care so much about Project Youth."

That I care so much about Project Youth? Bruce stared at her blankly. He knew what she was really saying: "That you care so much about *me.*" *I wasn't thinking about Pamela when I came up with this idea,* he realized with a stab of guilt. *I wasn't even thinking about Project Youth! I was thinking about . . .*

"Well, I guess I'll see you at the meeting," Bruce remarked, looking desperately for a way to make a quick getaway.

But Pamela kept a firm grip on his arm. "Hey, what happened to you last night?" she asked conversationally. "I thought we were going to go out for pizza or something. When I called your house, Roger had no idea where you were."

"I totally forgot," Bruce had to admit. "I . . . um . . . actually, I had dinner at Elizabeth and Jessica's. The house felt so empty—I had to get out of there."

The glow faded from Pamela's face. "Oh. Well, if you're ever lonely, you're always welcome over at my house. I mean, it goes without saying."

"Yeah," Bruce said lamely. "It was kind of an accident. I bumped into Wilkins, and we just ended up at the Wakefields'," he fibbed. "I mean, it wasn't like a date or anything."

Pamela looked surprised. "No, of course it wasn't. So, how about today, after school? Want to go to the beach?"

Bruce thought about Elizabeth and their plan to do some sleuthing at the university. "I've got some stuff to do," he replied evasively.

Pamela waited, obviously expecting him to elaborate. When he didn't, she pulled her arm away, her eyes shadowed with hurt. "OK." She shrugged. "Catch you later."

Without another word, she pivoted and walked off in the opposite direction. Bruce watched her go, a strange mix of emotions battling in his heart. *When was the last time I wanted more than anything to kiss her?* he wondered suddenly.

He felt a pang of remorse for being less than honest with her, but only a brief one. *She shouldn't put pressure on me, that's all. She doesn't own me. I can do what I want, see who I want. We're not married, after all!*

Maria Santelli folded her arms on top of the lunch table and fixed sparkling dark eyes on Jessica. "OK, Wakefield. Winston's been hinting that some kind of hanky-panky's going on at your house while your parents are away. What's the scoop?"

"Hanky-panky? At *my* house?" Jessica sounded shocked. "Never. You must have gotten the story wrong."

"C'mon," Maria insisted, "tell us what's going on!"

Jessica glanced around the table at the curious faces of her friends. *If I tell Maria and Amy and Jeanie and Robin, and they each tell four people, and those four people each tell four people . . . But if Todd already told Winston, I can certainly tell my friends.*

"It's really not that exciting," she told Maria and the others. "Todd's parents are out of town too, so he and Liz are having a week-long slumber party."

Four pairs of wide eyes stared at Jessica. "No way!" Jeanie squeaked. "He's sleeping over with your sister?"

Jessica hurried to defend Elizabeth's honor. "Of course they're not *sleeping* together. This is Elizabeth we're talking about! She relegated Todd to the downstairs couch—they're the king and queen of self-control, believe me."

124

"If that were me and Barry . . . !" Amy wiggled her eyebrows suggestively.

"Tell them about last night, Jess," Lila prompted.

Jessica obliged, describing how Bruce and then Lila had crashed the romantic dinner Todd was preparing for Elizabeth. "Bruce?" Robin asked.

"Yeah," Jessica said. "All of a sudden he's Elizabeth's new best friend. Actually, I'm starting to get the impression that there's something going on between the two of them."

"You're kidding!" exclaimed Jeanie. "But what about Todd?"

"And what about Pamela?" demanded Maria. "I thought she and Bruce—"

At that moment Amy elbowed Maria sharply in the side. Twisting in her chair to follow the direction of Amy's gaze, Jessica quickly saw the reason why.

Pamela stood a few feet away, a lunch tray in her hands and a shy smile on her face. "Is there room for one more?" she asked.

"Of course!" Lila answered Pamela, sliding her chair to one side.

"Have a seat," Robin urged.

Pamela squeezed in between Lila and Jeanie. "So, what's up?" she asked conversationally.

"Nothing at all," replied Maria.

"Absolutely nothing," Amy confirmed. "We were just talking about . . . What *were* we talking about?"

"I don't remember," said Jessica.

"Me, either," Robin contributed.

Pamela unwrapped her sandwich, a sudden wave of insecurity making her toes curl in her shoes. "Guess I haven't missed much, then," she said, forcing a light laugh.

"You really haven't," Maria assured her. "It's a quiet day on the grapevine."

A quiet day on the grapevine . . . *They were talking about me when I walked up,* Pamela deduced, taking a bite of her sandwich.

She remembered her first days at Sweet Valley High. Walking down the strange hallways had been like running a gauntlet. Her reputation as a girl who "put out" had preceded her from Big Mesa; whenever she entered a room, all talk would cease and kids put their heads together to start whispering.

But these girls are my friends now, Pamela reminded herself. *They wouldn't talk about me behind my back.* What was it, then, that had caused them to clam up when she joined the group?

As if in answer to her question, Pamela glanced toward the cafeteria door just as Bruce entered with Elizabeth. The two stood side by side in the lunch line, talking and laughing. Studying them out of the corner of her eye, Pamela chewed slowly, her sandwich suddenly tasting like sawdust. *Is that what the girls were talking about? No. It can't be. I'm just being paranoid.*

"I heard there's a sale at Lisette's," Jessica

burst out. "Who wants to go shopping with me this afternoon?"

"I do," said Lila. "I need a new bathing suit."

"I've been looking for some dressy sandals," Maria chimed in. "How 'bout you, Pam? Want to go to the mall?"

"Sure." Pamela did her best to appear nonchalant—and to *feel* nonchalant. "Any place that's air-conditioned!"

Todd slouched down the hall after the final bell, listening as a voice announced over the P.A. system that all sports were canceled that afternoon because of the hot weather. He stopped at the water fountain. When he looked up, Aaron Dallas waved at him from the other side of the crowded corridor. "What's up, Wilkins?" Aaron called.

Todd joined his friend. "Not a lot."

"Something must be up," Aaron remarked as they walked toward their lockers together. "I've been calling your house all week, but you're never home."

Todd figured the truth, or part of it, couldn't hurt. At this point, he didn't care who knew. "My folks are out of town, and so are Elizabeth's," he told Aaron. "We're spending a little more time together than usual, if you know what I mean."

Aaron gave Todd a hearty slap on the back. "That's right. I heard you were camping out over there."

Todd laughed. "I should have known Winston and Bill would blab."

"Can't blame them," Aaron said with a grin. "So, a bunch of the guys are heading over to Secca Lake for a swim this afternoon, since sports are canceled. What do you say?"

A swim at Secca Lake . . . It was a pretty attractive proposition. *And I haven't hung out with my friends all week,* Todd realized. "I've got plans with Liz," Todd said a little remorsefully, even though they hadn't actually made any yet.

"It's not necessarily a guys-only thing. Bring her," suggested Aaron.

Todd halted at his locker. "Maybe we'll see you there."

"Sure. Catch you later," Aaron said with a salute.

Todd watched his friend saunter off, wondering if he'd made the right call. *Liz and I don't have to do everything together,* he thought. *We lead our own lives—it's always been that way.* Slamming his locker shut, he took a step to follow Aaron, then stopped. *But this week was supposed to be different,* he reminded himself. *It's supposed to be about togetherness.*

Todd nodded, sure of himself again. And yet, for some reason, a feeling of isolation dogged him as he headed toward Elizabeth's locker to take one more shot at togetherness.

Chapter 11

When the final bell rang, Elizabeth hurried straight to the student parking lot without stopping at her locker first. She didn't want to run into anybody—she didn't want anyone to know where she was going.

Bruce was waiting for her by his black Porsche. When he spotted Elizabeth, he opened the passenger door, and she slid into the car as if she'd been doing it for years. "I'm glad you could come," he said simply, starting the engine.

"Me, too."

They roared off in the direction of the coast highway, heading north. *I shouldn't be in such a good mood,* Elizabeth thought, glancing at Bruce out of the corner of her eye. After all, they had a pretty depressing motive for paying a visit to the college campus where their parents had been students a few decades earlier. But for some reason, she did feel good, lighthearted and liberated.

Bruce looked over. Catching her eye, he smiled. "Feels like we're playing hooky, huh?"

Elizabeth laughed. "I don't know why, but it does. Maybe because . . ." She hesitated, and then decided to make a full confession. "Maybe because I didn't tell Todd where I was going."

"I didn't tell Pamela, either," said Bruce. "Face it, they just wouldn't understand."

Elizabeth tried to explain herself. "Todd wants me to lean on him. He wants to be there for me. But it's not that easy. Sometimes I can't even find the words to explain to him how all this makes me feel."

"I know exactly what you mean," Bruce assured her.

Elizabeth gazed at his profile as he drove. *You do know*, she thought. *That's why I like being with you.*

Suddenly Jessica's startling question from the night before popped into Elizabeth's head. *"What's going on with you and Bruce?"* Elizabeth turned her face away so Bruce couldn't see the pink color creeping up in her cheeks. She'd answered Jessica promptly, and in the negative. But maybe that had been a lie, Elizabeth realized now, her pulse racing.

As they turned into the palm-tree-lined drive leading to the university's main quadrangle, Bruce slowed the car. "Where should we go first?" he asked Elizabeth.

She pointed to a large, central building with massive white pillars. "The library. They'll have archives with old student newspapers and things like that."

Bruce and Elizabeth sat side by side at microfilm machines in the basement of the library. Elizabeth whirled the knob on her machine, squinting at the tiny print.

"Here's something!" Bruce exclaimed after a moment. "It's about pledge week at the fraternities and sororities. Here's a picture of guys in jackets and ties having scotch and cigars at my dad's fraternity house—and there's ol' Hank!"

Elizabeth peeked over Bruce's shoulder. "So much for ol' Hank being a tie-dyed hippie radical," she commented.

Bruce pointed to the date. "But this was a whole year before the sit-in. There was plenty of time to grow his hair and change his attitude!"

Elizabeth returned to her screen and gave the knob another spin. A headline caught her eye. "'Big Turnout at First "Women for Peace" Meeting,'" she read out loud. "Hey, according to this article, my mother was a founding member of the group."

"'Women for Peace,' huh? No doubt about *her* politics," Bruce joked.

Elizabeth skimmed another article. "Listen to this one," she said. "'The Board of Trustees announced yesterday that Professor Yarovitch, a prominent civil-rights activist, has been suspended from the faculty without pay. Students for Progressive

Action Now (SPAN), the largest antiwar/civil-rights organization on campus, has thrown its full support behind Professor Yarovitch and promises a mammoth demonstration on his behalf.'"

"The sit-in!" Bruce said.

"Right." Eagerly Elizabeth moved on to the next day's paper. "Look at this picture. There must've been a thousand kids involved!"

Bruce slid his chair closer to Elizabeth's. "See your mom anywhere?"

Elizabeth shook her head. It was impossible to tell—any one of the long-haired girls could have been Alice Robertson.

Reaching an arm around Elizabeth, Bruce sped forward a day. "Here's the clipping we found in your mother's trunk," he said. "The story about Dad and the food drop."

Bruce and Elizabeth read the article again, their faces close together. "I get the feeling the person who wrote this was just as surprised as we were at the role your father played," Elizabeth mused.

Bruce whistled in disbelief. "What did he have to gain? He could have gotten in trouble with the administration—he could've been kicked out of school."

"He must've been like the rest of the kids," Elizabeth surmised. "He believed in the cause."

"I guess so." Bruce wrinkled his forehead. "I'm just trying to figure him out. I mean, in general we're a lot alike. But could the cause really have been what drove him?"

"Maybe there are some answers here." Elizabeth focused the screen on a story dated a week after the sit-in. "It's an interview with your dad."

"'Campus Hero Shares Vision of the Future.'" Bruce laughed. "This is just too funny."

"No, it's serious," Elizabeth said, reading the article with interest. "Your father sounds really sincere. Listen to this: 'I think for too long people have allowed themselves to be separated by labels like "radical" and "conservative," "rich" and "poor," "black" and "white," "young" and "old." We can't afford to let such gaps keep us apart and diminish our strength. If we want to enact change, we need to band together.'"

For a moment they sat quietly, absorbing the significance of the words Hank Patman had uttered long ago, years before Elizabeth and Bruce were even born. "I didn't understand it before, but now I can see why my mom was drawn to your father," Elizabeth said softly. "I see why she admired him." Their arms were touching, and she could feel the heat of his skin through his shirt sleeve.

All at once Elizabeth became intensely aware of Bruce's nearness. And when he looked at her that way, it was as if he were looking straight into her soul.

Elizabeth dropped her gaze, and Bruce rolled his chair back to the other microfilm machine. "I guess we found what we were looking for," he remarked, turning the knob. "Hey, wait!" He zeroed in on something. "It's the gossip page—there's a blurb about Alice Robertson and Hank Patman's engagement!"

Elizabeth read the short article. "They make it sound like a fairy tale."

Bruce gave her another one of those warm, penetrating looks. "Maybe it was," he said quietly.

The lower level of the library was dry and cool; nevertheless, Elizabeth's skin felt very hot. An electric current pulsed between her and Bruce, holding them close.

It's starting to make sense, why Mom and Mr. Patman fell in love, Elizabeth thought as she stood up and made a conscious effort to step away from Bruce. *And if Bruce is so much like his father, and I'm so much like my mother . . .*

"This campus is so beautiful," Elizabeth remarked as she and Bruce emerged from the library and strolled across the emerald-green quadrangle. "It must have been exciting to be a student here in the sixties. The big outdoor concerts and rallies— all that energy and emotion, all that *life*."

Bruce gazed at Elizabeth. A breeze ruffled her shimmering blond hair; her lips parted in a dreamy smile. *Energy, emotion, life . . . that's you, Elizabeth,* Bruce thought.

"Maybe they stood here." Elizabeth tapped her foot on the grass. "My mother and your father," she explained when Bruce gave her a blank look. "Walking to and from classes together, meeting each

134

other for lunch or a study break . . . This place." She lifted her arms to the sky. "This is where they . . ."

She didn't finish the sentence; she didn't have to. *This is where they fell in love.* Bruce felt the blood pumping fast through his veins. Suddenly he had an uncanny sensation. He felt close to his father's past. *I could almost be Dad,* he thought, *and Liz could be her mom.*

"Let's explore!" Bruce blurted. "Let's *see* where they lived and studied and went on dates."

Elizabeth's eyes lit up. Bruce could tell she was feeling the strange magic of this moment too. "Let's," she agreed.

Running back to the library to grab a campus map, Bruce and Elizabeth plotted out a nostalgic tour. "Dad's fraternity house," Bruce said, indicating a building on the west side of campus.

Elizabeth pointed to another site. "Mom's freshman dorm!"

They found the dormitory first. "I have no idea which room was hers," said Elizabeth, climbing the steps to read the sign in the lobby. "Looks like the girls' rooms are on the second and third floors. Let's just take a look."

The second floor was a lively place. Many of the students had their doors propped open, and music poured into the hallway—an eclectic blend of rock, reggae, and rap. At a bend in the corridor, a girl chatted on the hall phone. "It smells like popcorn," Bruce observed.

135

"And hair spray," Elizabeth said with a giggle.

They paused by the room nearest to the stairwell. The door was ajar; Elizabeth peeked in, Bruce looking over her shoulder. There were books and clothes everywhere, potted plants that looked as if they hadn't been watered in a year, a stereo, a desktop computer, tapestries and movie-star posters on the walls, and stuffed animals on the bed.

Elizabeth smiled, a faraway look in her eyes. "I can kind of see her here, you know?" she said. "Sitting at that desk, writing that letter to your father . . ."

Bruce squinted, trying to summon up the same picture. "Me, too."

Someone cleared her throat behind them. Elizabeth and Bruce jumped. "Are you looking for someone?" the girl asked with a friendly smile.

She was blond, blue-eyed, and naturally beautiful in a fresh, all-American way. *An Alice Robertson type,* Bruce thought.

Elizabeth looked as if she'd turned around and found herself face-to-face with a phantom. "We're prospective freshmen," Bruce replied easily. "Just taking a self-guided tour. Didn't mean to snoop."

The girl laughed, slipping past them into her room. "No problem."

Bruce steered Elizabeth back toward the staircase. "I feel like they're still here, you know?" he said conspiratorially.

"Me, too."

The feeling grew stronger as they walked across the big, manicured lawn of Hank Patman's old fraternity house fifteen minutes later. *Now, this is college life!* Bruce thought. Classes were over for the day; it was time for serious R & R. Guys wearing sunglasses and no shirts lounging on lawn chairs; kids playing Frisbee while others tossed a football; a couple of boys working on getting a fire started in a grill.

Elizabeth pointed at a tall stack of empty pizza boxes on the porch of the house. "A typical male decorating scheme."

Bruce laughed.

"So, can you see your dad here?" she asked.

Bruce nodded. "Definitely."

They ended up in the coffee shop at the student union an hour later. Elizabeth bought a slice of pepperoni pizza; Bruce ordered a burger, onion rings, and a chocolate shake.

They carried their food outside and sat down on the broad steps. "No wonder we're so hungry," Bruce said, gesturing toward the western sky. The sun had dropped behind the palm trees, casting a golden light on the scene.

"I feel like we stepped out of time for a while," Elizabeth told him. "I never really thought much about my mother's life before I was born. But in the sixties, kids thought they could make a difference. Nowadays the problems just seem too big for us. We don't have the same kind of innocent confidence."

Ordinarily Bruce might have made some snide,

cynical comment: "Why should I care about the rest of the world's problems as long as *I'm* comfortable?" But Elizabeth's sincerity was contagious. Bruce didn't want to antagonize her; he wanted to please her, to be admired by her. He wanted her to look at him with those wide, shining eyes and nod and smile, as if they were the only two people in the world who shared an incredibly special secret.

"Oh, I don't know." Reaching out, Bruce took Elizabeth's hand in his. "I think you could do whatever you set your mind to."

They touched only for a moment, and then Bruce let go of Elizabeth's hand. Only for a moment . . . but it was a moment that seemed to last forever. Sparks crackled between them; Bruce stared at Elizabeth and she stared back at him. He had the craziest urge to follow the touch with a kiss.

The revelation struck Bruce like a lightning bolt. *If Dad could fall in love with Alice Robertson, why shouldn't I fall in love with her daughter?*

As they drove back toward Sweet Valley, Elizabeth was still tingling from the feel of Bruce's hand on hers. She was relieved when he slipped a CD in the car stereo; with music playing, they weren't obligated to talk.

It had been an afternoon of startling revelations. *What happened to us back there?* Elizabeth wondered, recalling the exhilaration that possessed her, the intimacy that connected her and Bruce. *It was as if our parents' pasts were our own memories,* Elizabeth realized, *like it was our story. Or maybe we're part of the story. It's still going on, it never really ended. Maybe Bruce and I are fated to be together, just like Mom and Mr. Patman!*

Elizabeth gripped her hands tightly in her lap, a wave of guilt and denial washing over her. Where would that leave Todd and Pamela, and Elizabeth's father and Mrs. Patman? Things were getting more complicated by the minute; it made her head spin.

She glanced sideways at Bruce. In the last light of the setting sun, with his black hair whipping in the wind, he looked dramatically handsome. Sensing her glance, he turned his head and flashed a smile, his blue eyes shooting out sparks. Elizabeth smiled back, her heart leaping. *That dimple in his chin . . . why haven't I ever noticed how incredibly gorgeous he is?* she wondered dizzily.

"Someone's had a breakdown," Bruce remarked as they rounded a bend in the road on the outskirts of town.

Elizabeth peered ahead in the dusk. A car was pulled over on the shoulder; a man stood next to it, waving. Bruce tapped the Porsche's brakes. "Might as well see if we can help."

As they neared the other car, however, Elizabeth wished they'd blown right by it. *It's Todd!* she realized with dismay.

Todd held his fist in the air, thumbing a ride. When he recognized the Porsche, he dropped his

139

hand. When he saw who was in the passenger seat, his eyes almost popped out of his head.

Bruce rolled down his window. "Climb on in."

After a moment's hesitation, Todd wedged himself into the Porsche's tiny backseat. Taking a deep breath, Elizabeth twisted around to give her boyfriend a feeble smile. "What happened to you?"

Todd stared at her. "My car broke down," he muttered. "What does it look like?"

Elizabeth swallowed. "I hope it's nothing serious," she said, trying to sound cheerful.

Todd continued to glare at her, his expression black and stormy. "I was starting to worry about you," he told her.

For some reason, she wasn't ready to tell the truth. "We were just . . . I needed a book from the university library, and Bruce, uh, Bruce gave me a lift."

I'm sure he sees right through me, she thought as she faced forward again. *I've never been a very good liar.* Suddenly a wave of indignation swept over her and she squared her shoulders defiantly. *How dare he put me on the spot like that! I don't owe him any explanation. He's just my boyfriend— he doesn't own me.*

"Where can I take you, Wilkins?" Bruce asked Todd as they neared downtown.

"Liz's . . . I guess," Todd said sulkily. "I'll call a tow truck from there."

Elizabeth gazed out the window at the rising

140

moon, hoping Todd could see how unconcerned she was about having been "caught" spending an afternoon with another boy. *Maybe we're "living together," but we're not married yet—and maybe we never will be.*

Chapter 12

The Porsche rolled to a stop in the Wakefields' driveway and Elizabeth climbed out. Todd emerged
from the cramped backseat, unfolding his long legs
stiffly. "Thanks for the lift," he grumbled, turning
toward the house.

Elizabeth lingered in the driveway. "Would you
like to come in?" Todd heard her ask Bruce.

I can't believe it! Todd thought, his annoyance
level rising to new heights. *Doesn't that guy ever
get the message?* But maybe that was the problem.
Todd clenched his jaw. *I'm sending one message,
but obviously Elizabeth's sending another.*

They found Jessica in the kitchen, boiling water
for spaghetti. Todd made a beeline for the phone,
grabbing the yellow pages on the way. He watched
Elizabeth and Bruce out of the corner of his eye
while he spoke to the towing company. "I'll call

them about it in the morning. Thanks."

Hanging up the phone, Todd joined the others.

"So," said Jessica, her eyes sparkling mischievously. "Here we are again. I guess I need to cook more spaghetti. Or should I turn it over to you, Todd?"

Todd stifled a groan, envisioning a rerun of the previous evening's fiasco.

Jessica started to hand the box of spaghetti to Todd, then drew it back. "On second thought, maybe we shouldn't let ourselves get into such a boring rut. I know. Let's go dancing!"

"It's a weeknight," Elizabeth reminded her sister.

Jessica burst out laughing. "That's the whole *point*. Mom and Dad aren't around to stop us!"

"But what if they call and we're out?" Elizabeth asked.

Jessica waved a hand. "We'll just explain that we were so busy doing our homework that we couldn't be bothered picking up the phone."

Elizabeth rolled her eyes. "Yeah, they'll believe that!"

"I'm up for it," Bruce chimed in. "There's no one home to check up on me, either."

"So, what do you say?" Jessica looked at Elizabeth and Todd. Todd looked at Elizabeth and Bruce. He liked the idea of dancing at the Beach Disco with Elizabeth, but how could he make sure that Bruce stayed out of the way? Inspiration struck. "Sounds like fun. Bruce, why don't you call

Pamela and see if she can meet us there?"

Bruce looked startled. "Uh, sure," he said, shooting a glance at Elizabeth. "I'll do that."

"Maybe I'll call some people too," Jessica decided. "The more the merrier!"

The more the merrier . . . yeah, right, Todd thought glumly as he danced with Jessica at the Beach Disco.

Jessica had managed to talk a bunch of people into sneaking out to join them. Lila, Amy, Pamela, Barry, Aaron, and Ken had all given their parents a story about going to a study group at the library. There were plenty of people for Bruce to dance with, including Bruce's own girlfriend. *So how come he keeps ending up on the dance floor with* my *girlfriend?* Todd wondered.

"Liz sure looks like she's having a good time," said Jessica, spinning Todd in a circle so he could get a better look. "That's a pretty hot dance Bruce is teaching her!"

Todd frowned, watching Bruce guide Elizabeth through the complicated Latin steps with a *lot* of body contact. Bruce whirled Elizabeth so that her back was to him, clasped her briefly in his arms, and then spun her out again at arm's length. Todd gritted his teeth, but Elizabeth didn't seem to mind. Her eyes sparkled like jewels as Bruce pulled her close again and whispered something in her ear, making her laugh.

144

Face it, it's not all Bruce's doing, Todd had to acknowledge to himself. Todd had claimed Elizabeth for all the slow dances, but in between them she kept giving him the slip, darting off to fast-dance with Barry or Ken or, most often, Bruce.

Jessica shimmied to the music, her eyes on her sister and Bruce. "They make a cute couple, don't they? I mean, not that they *are* a couple," she amended as Todd shot her a dirty look. "But if they were . . ."

The next song was a slow one. Still breathless from dancing with Elizabeth, Bruce joined Pamela, who'd been standing on the sidelines, watching the action.

He held out a hand, ready to pull her onto the dance floor. "It's OK. We don't have to," Pamela said, hanging back. "You look like you could stand to sit one out."

"But this is your favorite song," Bruce insisted.

Pamela bit her lip as Bruce hustled her onto the floor and then started swaying with her to the music.

She really couldn't figure out why Bruce had invited her out tonight. Clearly, he couldn't care less whether or not she had a good time. *He's dancing with me now because he has to,* Pamela thought. *Elizabeth is dancing with Todd.*

Pamela rested her cheek against Bruce's chest, stifling a sigh. Bruce was a complex person. She knew that. Lately, though, he was harder than ever to figure out, and she didn't think it was just because he was upset about his parents' separation. *The only thing I seem to be able to count on these days,* she thought unhappily, *is that if he's not home when I call, he's over at Elizabeth's.*

Lifting her head, she studied her boyfriend's face. Bruce was humming along to the song, his gaze wandering around the Beach Disco and his lips curved in a half-smile. *I know who he's thinking about,* Pamela thought sadly. But there was still one thing that Pamela suddenly found herself dying to know.

I might as well just ask, she decided, clearing her throat. "You've probably been to the Beach Disco about a million times in the past with different girls," she ventured, her tone casual.

"It's the only dance place around here," Bruce conceded.

"Did you ever date either of the Wakefield twins?" Pamela asked.

She held her breath, waiting for Bruce to see right through to her scared and jealous heart. But the question seemed to amuse him. "I went out with Jessica a bunch of times," he said with a wry smile. "Things might've gotten pretty hot between us . . . if we hadn't realized we couldn't stand each other."

Pamela laughed. "What about Elizabeth? Did you ever date her?"

Bruce shook his head, his glance flickering over to Todd and Elizabeth. "Nope."

"Did you ever want to?" Pamela pressed, hating to ask such pathetic questions but desperately needing to know the truth.

Bruce shook his head again. "I never thought she was my type."

Pamela couldn't help noticing the past tense. "But now . . ." Her face turned beet-red.

Bruce scowled, his arms tensing around her. "What are you getting at, Pamela?"

Pamela bit her lip, flustered. "It just seems like—I get the feeling that . . ." Her voice trailed off; tears sprang to her eyes.

Bruce didn't comfort her; he didn't swear that he loved her and no one else. Instead, he stared at her hard, his blue eyes cold and distant. "Liz is fun to be with," he said flatly.

The implication being that I'm not. Pamela blinked back more tears, wishing with all her heart that she'd just stayed at home. "I'm—I'm sorry," she whispered. "You just don't seem happy with me anymore. What am I doing wrong?"

"Just chill out, Pamela," Bruce said. "Everything's fine."

The slow song continued, and Bruce pulled her close, ending the conversation. Pamela held on to him tightly, trying to take comfort from his embrace. But it was no use. Their bodies were pressed together, but Bruce's mind and heart were a thousand miles away.

∗   ∗   ∗

147

"This must be the long version of this song," said Elizabeth, a trace of impatience in her voice, as she slow-danced with Todd.

"I hope it lasts forever," Todd murmured, wrapping her more tightly in his arms.

Elizabeth, however, couldn't wait for it to end. Tonight every slow song felt like a chore; she resented having to go off in search of Todd whenever the tempo slowed.

I'm tired of him, Elizabeth recognized, shocked at herself for having such a thought. *I love him, but I'm tired of this week, of this let's-pretend-we're-married game.* It had been so refreshing to escape that afternoon and go off adventuring with Bruce. Bruce . . .

Overcome with guilt, Elizabeth nestled closer to Todd. *I can't believe I'm thinking about another guy while I'm dancing with Todd!* Elizabeth chastised herself. She couldn't deny it, though. She'd been thinking about Bruce ever since he had taken her hand that afternoon. What would it be like to dance like this with Bruce—to have *his* arms around her?

The slow song faded out, and an irresistibly fast beat began pulsing over the sound system. Elizabeth took a step away from Todd just as Bruce called out to her. "Hey, Liz, I want to show you some more samba steps!"

Something strange is happening to me, Elizabeth thought as she floated eagerly to Bruce's side.

148

She had a feeling that the smart thing to do, the practical thing, would be to get some distance from both Todd and Bruce, get some perspective. Instead, she continued to whirl from one boy to the other, tumbling deeper and deeper into a well of confusing, frightening, intoxicating new feelings.

Taking a break from the action, Jessica, Lila, Amy, Barry, and Aaron carried their tall glasses of foamy, frosty fruit drinks to a table with a view of the dance floor. "I really can't believe my eyes," Lila drawled, tugging at the hem of her black Lycra miniskirt. "Elizabeth Wakefield is hanging all over Bruce Patman. Or maybe he's hanging all over her. One or the other."

"And while she's 'living' with Todd!" exclaimed Barry.

"Hey, how'd you find out about that?" Jessica demanded. "Did you tell him, Amy?"

Amy lifted her shoulders helplessly. "Sorry, Jess. But I figured everyone knew at this point."

"Well, she and Bruce are just *dancing*," Jessica pointed out in a halfhearted attempt to preserve her sister's reputation. "It's not like they're making out or anything."

"You wouldn't know that from Wilkins's expression," observed Aaron.

Jessica and the others focused on Todd, who was keeping an eagle-eye on Elizabeth and Bruce from the opposite side of the dance floor.

"Meanwhile, poor Pamela's hiding in the bath-room," said Amy.

"Do you seriously think Liz is interested in Bruce?" Lila asked Jessica.

"I was just joking about it at first, yanking Todd's chain," Jessica replied. "But now I don't know. She says she's not, but look at them!"

They all watched as Bruce wrapped his arms around Elizabeth and dipped her backward. "From the Videomat to this in just two nights," Lila commented.

"And right under Pam's and Todd's noses!" said Amy.

Jessica couldn't help grinning at this ironic twist of fate. "My sister, the wildest girl at Sweet Valley High!"

"That was so much fun," said Jessica as she, Todd, and Elizabeth piled into the Jeep. "I can't believe we haven't been going out every night!"

Todd shifted gears without commenting.

"We still have the weekend," Elizabeth pointed out.

"I know!" Jessica exclaimed. "Saturday night, let's throw a big bash at the house!"

"We could have a pool party," Elizabeth said enthusiastically, "since this heat wave's still on."

"We'll invite everyone," said Jessica.

Todd opened his mouth to remind Elizabeth that Saturday would be their last night of living together, then thought better of it. *She wouldn't care,* he realized. *She'd just accuse me of being a bore, which maybe I am.*

Back at the house, Jessica grabbed a glass of water from the kitchen and headed upstairs. "See ya in the morning," she called over her shoulder. "And, Todd? How about omelets for breakfast tomorrow?"

Todd didn't have the energy to put up even token resistance. "Sure, Jessica."

Elizabeth helped Todd unfold the sofa bed, and then they stood for a moment, their arms wrapped around each other in a good-night hug. Suddenly Todd felt wistful and even a little scared. Their week was almost over. . . . *And instead of bringing us closer, it's driven a wedge between us.* "Good night, Elizabeth," Todd whispered.

"Night," she said, her voice empty of emotion.

He could almost feel Elizabeth pushing him away . . . even as she closed her eyes and lifted her face automatically for a kiss.

Chapter 13

"I'm so glad it's finally Friday," Elizabeth exclaimed as she spread out her beach towel. "I feel like a prisoner about to be released from jail!"

Enid jabbed the pole of the beach umbrella into the sand. "Not a very good commentary on Todd, I'd say."

"You're right." Elizabeth sat down in the shade of the umbrella. Wrapping her arms around her knees, she gazed out over the ocean. "Enid . . ."

Enid opened the cooler to take out two icy cans of soda and handed one to her friend, looking at Elizabeth expectantly.

"This is going to give you a terrible impression of me, but I have to talk about it," Elizabeth began. "Last night a bunch of us went out dancing and . . ."

"And what?" Enid prompted when Elizabeth fell silent.

Elizabeth's face flamed a bright tomato-red. "And when I was dancing with Bruce, I . . . I liked it," she confessed. "I liked it better than dancing with Todd."

"That's not so terrible," Enid said with a smile.

Elizabeth gazed earnestly at her friend. "You mean, you don't think it's sleazy and rotten to have feelings for Bruce when I'm going out with Todd?"

"It all depends on what you do about those feelings," Enid replied.

Elizabeth rested her cheek on her tucked-up knees, sighing heavily. "I just never expected anything like this to happen when Todd moved in at the beginning of the week!"

"Have you tried talking things over with Todd?"

"What would I say? 'You're driving me nuts, and by the way, I can't stop thinking about Bruce Patman'?"

Enid laughed again. "Maybe you could try a more subtle approach."

"Tell me what you'd do if you were me," Elizabeth begged.

Enid stretched out her slim, lightly tanned legs, burrowing her toes in the sand. "If I were you, I'd give Todd one more chance," she said after a moment of thoughtful silence. "I mean, Bruce is a distraction, but maybe if you try to focus on your relationship with Todd, the two of you can figure out what went wrong this week."

Elizabeth nodded. "You're right," she admitted.

"I don't know why, but I've been shutting Todd out. I want to make it work with him," she said softly. "I don't like feeling so confused."

Enid patted Elizabeth's arm. "You'll figure things out."

With another deep sigh, Elizabeth lay back on her beach towel. *Will I?* she wondered.

"I'm ready when you are," Roger called to Bruce from the upstairs hallway on Friday evening.

Bruce's mother had invited the two boys to dinner at her new house. "Be right there," Bruce yelled back.

Standing in front of the mirror over his dresser, he tucked the tails of his polo shirt into his khakis and ran a comb through his damp hair. Sticking his bare feet into a pair of scuffed loafers, he headed for the door and then stopped. Pivoting, he returned to his bedside table to dial a telephone number.

Pamela answered after just one ring. "Hope you weren't sitting by the phone waiting for me to call," Bruce kidded.

"Don't flatter yourself," Pamela joked back. "What's up?"

"I'm on my way to my mom's new place—just wanted to say hi. Also I wanted to see if . . ." Bruce hesitated. "If you'd like to come with me to Elizabeth and Jessica's pool party tomorrow night."

"Do you really want me to?" Pamela countered, sounding uncertain.

"Of course I do," he said with false heartiness. "It's Saturday night—we're always together on Saturday night."

"As long as you're sure you want to be together, that it's not just a habit we've gotten into," said Pamela.

"I want to," Bruce repeated. "I'll pick you up at seven."

"Great. I—I love you, Bruce."

He could hear the relief in her voice, knew exactly what she was thinking. *Last night at the Beach Disco was awkward, but it's going to be all right.*

"Yeah. I love you, too, Pamela."

"Hot dogs and hamburgers," Jessica murmured at midday on Saturday, scribbling the words on a pad of paper.

"Buns," contributed Todd, pulling up a chair at the kitchen table.

"Drinks," said Elizabeth, fanning herself with a magazine. "Soda, lemonade, juice."

"Plastic cups, paper plates, plastic forks, pretzels, chips . . ." Jessica continued to write madly. "How about ice cream?"

Elizabeth shook her head. "Too drippy—it would melt before we could even serve it."

"We need something cool, though," said Jessica, plucking an ice cube from her glass and sliding it across her forehead.

"Fruit salad," Todd suggested. "Buy a big watermelon and carve it out into a boat and then fill it up again with melon balls, grapes, berries, stuff like that."

"Perfect!" Elizabeth beamed at Todd. "Mmm, my mouth's watering just thinking about it."

Todd shrugged. "As long as you don't mind a few watermelon seeds on the patio."

Jessica grinned. "That's OK with me, since cleaning up after the pool party will be Todd's last chore!"

"Finally, my week of indentured servitude is almost over," Todd kidded with a groan.

Elizabeth smiled, the sentiment echoing in her mind.

And maybe it's going to end up OK, she thought, recalling her chat with Enid. Todd was being a good sport about the pool party—the three of them were having fun planning it. *Maybe things will get back to normal between us next week,* Elizabeth anticipated. *He'll go home, and Mom and Dad will get back . . .*

Then she remembered. Things couldn't get back to normal. Her mom was probably going to come home only to announce that her marriage was a sham and she was moving in with Mr. Patman. And Bruce . . . No matter how hard she tried to focus on Todd and Todd alone, she couldn't help wondering. *What about Bruce?*

Jessica capped the pen and pushed her chair back. "OK, who's ready to shop?" she asked.

Todd hopped to his feet and gave her a salute. "Lead the way, *mon capitaine.*"

Laughing, they headed for the door. Just as Elizabeth was stepping into the garage, the phone rang. Turning back, she picked up the receiver.

The voice on the other end of the line sent a shiver racing up her spine. "Elizabeth? It's Bruce."

"Hi, Bruce," she said brightly. "What's up?"

"Not a lot," Bruce confessed. "I'm just kicking around with nothing to do, and I wondered if you guys needed help setting up for the party."

"Actually, we're on our way out the door right now to make a big shopping expedition," Elizabeth told him. "Want to come?"

"Sure," Bruce said. "Want to swing by and pick me up, or should I meet you at the store?"

"We'll come by your house," Elizabeth offered. "It's on the way. See you in five!"

Hanging up the phone, she hurried to rejoin Todd and Jessica. Jessica was already in the Jeep. Todd, meanwhile, stood in the garage just beyond the open door, his arms folded across his chest and a sharp frown line creasing his forehead.

"That was Bruce," Elizabeth started to explain. "He offered to help with the party, so I—"

"We heard," Todd snapped.

Elizabeth blinked at his abrupt tone. "Do you have a problem with that?" she asked coolly.

"Yes, I have a problem with it!" Todd exploded. "Why do we need him around?"

"We have a list as long as my leg of things to do!"

"There's just not room for him in the Jeep,"

Todd persisted. "Once we buy all that stuff—"

Elizabeth threw up her hands. Enid had advised her to be sensitive, but this was just more than she could take. She'd had it once and for all with Todd's possessive clinginess. "That's it, Todd," Elizabeth exclaimed. "I don't know what you thought living together would be like, but if making all the rules and controlling my every move is what you had in mind, you were way off base. Please remember, this is *my* house and *my* party! Maybe there *isn't* room for a fourth person in the Jeep—maybe you should stay home!"

Todd and Elizabeth glowered at each other. "If that's the way you feel about it, then I will stay home," he retorted.

Elizabeth brushed past him, stomping toward the Jeep, where a wide-eyed Jessica sat behind the wheel, drinking up every word. "Fine!" Elizabeth shouted.

"Fine!" Todd hurled after her.

Todd slurped a glass of iced tea and glared through the sliding glass door from the kitchen to the Wakefields' backyard. Elizabeth and Jessica had positioned the stereo speakers so they were pointing out the windows, and they bustled about on the patio to the rocking rhythms of Jamie Peters's latest smash CD.

While Jessica strung Japanese lanterns from the trees, Elizabeth and Bruce splashed around in the pool, supposedly in order to set up a water volleyball net. "At this rate, it'll take them the rest of the afternoon and half the night," Todd muttered, as Bruce dove underwater and playfully pulled Elizabeth under.

The sun had dropped in the sky, but the heat was still unbearable; the air was thick and heavy. In the distance, thunder rumbled ominously. *A storm's coming—maybe the heat will finally break*, Todd thought. In the pool, Bruce lifted Elizabeth onto his shoulders so she could dunk the volleyball over the net. Todd stood up abruptly, knocking over his iced tea.

I've had it, Todd fumed, grabbing a sponge to mop up the spilled tea. He'd had it with Elizabeth's careless disregard of his feelings, with her flirting with another guy right under his nose. One thing was certain. *Elizabeth is going to have to make up her mind*, Todd determined, his eyes still fixed on the pair in the swimming pool. *Either she's in this relationship with me, or she's out.*

159

Chapter 14

"Awesome music," Dana Larson raved to Elizabeth. Raising her arms over her head, Dana did a little shimmy, her metallic-green bikini glinting in the light of the Japanese lanterns. "I thought I was the only person who liked this band!"

"Bruce loaned us his CD collection," Elizabeth explained with a laugh. "I think he buys every record that comes out." Someone touched Elizabeth's arm, and she spun around.

"Just wanted to say hi to the hostess with the mostess," Olivia greeted her.

Enid and Hugh were there too, and Patty Gilbert and Jim Hollis. "Liz, that's the cutest outfit!" Patty exclaimed.

Elizabeth twirled so they could appreciate it from every angle. "I don't know if you can call a bathing suit with a piece of cloth tied around your waist an 'outfit,'" she said, laughing, "but thanks."

"You look like a tropical princess," Hugh said gallantly.

"This is a great party," Enid added, fending off Hugh's attempt to toss her into the pool. "I hope you're having as much fun as everybody else is."

"Oh, I am," Elizabeth assured her.

Elizabeth surveyed the scene in her backyard. The pool party *was* an unqualified success. *Food, drink, music, a pool, and a crowd of kids in bathing suits—with those ingredients, we really couldn't miss!*

There was only one sour note to the evening, and Elizabeth had decided she wasn't going to pay attention to it. At the other end of the patio, Todd was lighting a fire in the grill and sulking like a baby without a bottle. *I refuse to let him spoil my fun,* she decided, pointedly heading in the opposite direction to mingle with some newly arrived friends.

I don't need a guilt trip, she thought, waving at Ken and Terri and blowing an exaggerated kiss to Winston, who was wearing big baggy swim trunks with pouty red lips printed all over them.

As a rowdy volleyball game got started in the swimming pool, Bruce and Pamela walked around the side of the house and stepped onto the patio. Bruce's eyes moved right to Elizabeth, as if drawn by a magnet.

Even from a distance, she could see his eyes light up with pleasure at the sight of her. Elizabeth smiled back, more glad than ever that she'd borrowed Jessica's sexy tropical-print bikini and sarong.

161

For an instant, as Bruce held her gaze, time stood still. The noise and activity ceased, the other bodies dissolved, and there was just the two of them, silently communicating with their eyes across the distance that lay between them.

Why couldn't this have been someone else's pool party? Pamela wondered as she watched her boyfriend lift a hand to wave at Elizabeth.

"I need to greet our hostess," Bruce said, dropping the arm that had been loosely draped around Pamela's shoulders. "Be right back."

Pamela shrugged. "Sure." What else could she say?

As she watched Bruce hurry to Elizabeth's side, she tried to convince herself that his eagerness was perfectly innocent. *He's just being polite.* But reasoning didn't make her feel any better. When Bruce had called the night before to ask her to the party, the anxious knot in Pamela's stomach had dissolved. Now it was back, flooding her heart with agonizing doubt.

Spotting Lila, who was just arriving at the party, Pamela rushed to intercept her. "Lila!" she cried. "I've got to talk to you."

Lila smiled. "About what?"

"You've got to be one hundred percent honest with me," Pamela pleaded. "I've got a feeling everybody knows something I don't."

"Are you talking about Todd and Elizabeth living together?"

162

"No, I heard about that," said Pamela. "It's something else. About Bruce. About Bruce and another girl." She put her hand on Lila's arm. "What's going on?"

Lila pursed her lips, her brown eyes narrowed thoughtfully. "I'm not sure what, if anything, is going on," she said, choosing her words with care. "A rumor or two is making the rounds. But the person to ask about all this," she concluded softly, "is Bruce."

"So, what do you want to do?" Bruce asked Pamela as they met up by a card table crowded with snacks and drinks. "Eat? Dance? Swim?"

"All three eventually," Pamela replied. "Let's just relax and hang out for a while, though."

"Sure." Bruce filled two cups with soda and handed her one. "Whatever."

His disinterest was audible. "Look, I don't have you on a tether," she said with a brittle laugh. "You can do whatever you like. Don't worry about entertaining me."

"You're my date, aren't you? We came together, we'll stay together."

Pamela bit her lip. After a quick glance around, she tugged on Bruce's arm. "Bruce, can we talk?"

"About what?"

"About us."

Bruce groaned. "Pamela, we're at a party, for heaven's sake. Can't it wait?"

163

"No." Pamela's voice was shaky, but her words were firm. "It can't."

Bruce let her pull him aside. "So, what's on your mind that's of such earth-shattering importance?" he asked impatiently.

"Elizabeth Wakefield."

Startled by the blunt reply, Bruce straightened, his gaze fixed on Pamela's face. "What *about* Elizabeth?"

"You have feelings for her, don't you?" Pamela challenged him.

If he'd had more time to think, Bruce probably would have been able to come up with a flip, dismissive answer. But Pamela had caught him unaware. He realized that he had to admit the truth—both to her, and to himself.

"Yes," Bruce stated simply. "I do."

Tears flooded Pamela's eyes and spilled over, running in two streams down her pale cheeks. "I never thought I'd hear you say that," she whispered. "I thought we were going to love each other forever."

Bruce stared at her, his own eyes smarting. That's what he'd thought too. He'd never cared for a girl the way he cared for Pamela. But now . . . "I still love you, Pamela," he said hoarsely.

She shook her head vehemently. "That word meant something once—please don't use it now if you don't mean it."

"Pamela." Bruce put his hands on her slender shoulders, gripping them tightly. "Don't do this."

"I'm not doing anything," she pointed out, tears

still streaming down her face. "You're the one who's forcing a change. I'm just giving you what you want."

"What's that?"

"Your freedom," Pamela whispered. Twisting out of his grasp, she darted off before he could stop her.

And I don't want to stop her, Bruce realized. Pamela's leaving wrenched his heart, but at the same time, he felt energized, liberated.

Overhead, a full yellow moon winked at him through the haze; heat lightning flickered but kept its distance. *When one thing ends, something new can begin,* he thought as his eyes raked the party, searching. He knew who he was looking for.

Elizabeth pulled another jar of salsa from the refrigerator. She didn't realize anyone had entered the kitchen until she turned and found Bruce standing only a few feet away.

"Oh!" she yelped. "Bruce, you scared me." She put a hand to her heart with a laugh. "I didn't think anyone saw me sneak in here."

"I thought you might need some help."

"There's not much to do at this point but keep restocking the snacks." Elizabeth pointed to a platter. "If you load that up with veggies and dip, I'll zap another batch of nachos in the microwave."

"It's a great party," Bruce remarked as he spooned some dip into the small bowl. "Everyone's having a blast."

She tipped her head to one side, smiling at him. "Including you?"

His blue eyes twinkled as he smiled back. "Yes, including me."

"I'm glad," Elizabeth said sincerely. "I feel like this is a big night for us, you know?"

Putting down the spoon, Bruce took a step in her direction. "A big night—in what way?"

"It's been such a crazy week," Elizabeth explained. "And in the weeks to come . . . well, things may only get crazier. My mom gets home tomorrow, and so does my dad. I can't help wondering what's going to happen next."

"You're right. Everything in our world could change," Bruce agreed somberly. "But some things could change for the better."

Elizabeth sighed. "I suppose. But I'm scared, Bruce," she confessed. "I'm terrified. Maybe that's why tonight, I just want to go wild. I don't want to think about anything, I just want to—to—"

She stumbled to a stop, unable to find the right words.

"To live," Bruce suggested. "That's how I feel, anyway."

Elizabeth's eyes shone. "Yes, to live."

Bruce leaned back against the counter. "I'd be happy if this night never ended. I don't want to be there when my dad gets back from Chicago tomorrow and finds all Mom's stuff gone." Elizabeth saw his jaw tighten. "I'm afraid he won't even care—

I'm afraid he'll be glad. And meanwhile, she's all alone in that house."

Bruce's voice broke and his eyes reddened with unshed tears. "Oh, Bruce," Elizabeth said softly, sliding over to give him a comforting hug. "I'm sorry."

Bruce slipped his arms around her waist, burying his face in her hair. "Oh, Liz," he murmured, his lips warm against the bare skin of her neck.

Suddenly Elizabeth realized with a start that she was holding Bruce Patman in her arms, and that they were both wearing next to nothing. The skin of his back was bare and smooth under her hands, and he was kissing her neck. . . .

"Bruce!" Elizabeth gasped, too surprised to pull away. Bruce's mouth had found hers; he kissed her passionately, over and over. "Bruce," she said again, but this time her voice was low and eager. As Bruce's mouth pressed insistently on hers, Elizabeth began to kiss him back. She pulled him closer, her fingers sliding up his back to his shoulders and neck, tangling in his hair.

Suddenly Elizabeth's whole body tensed. For one impulsive, wildly emotional moment, she'd forgotten where she was. *What am I doing?* she thought dizzily.

Bracing her hands against Bruce's chest, she prepared to push him away from her. That was when Elizabeth saw Todd in the doorway, staring at them in horror.

Chapter 15

Todd froze. He wished he could go back in time and decide to stay out by the pool instead of follow Elizabeth into the house.

He couldn't go back, though. Obviously he'd been fated to walk into the kitchen at this very moment, to catch Elizabeth in someone else's arms.

Todd watched as Elizabeth and Bruce scrambled apart. It seemed to take forever for Elizabeth to straighten her sarong and shove back her tousled blond hair, and for Bruce's face to flush a hot, guilty red.

"Bruce," Elizabeth said after an agonizingly long and awkward moment, "would you leave us alone, please?"

Bruce put a hand on her arm, then dropped it. He glanced at Todd, then shifted his gaze away.

"I'll be outside if . . ." he muttered, not finishing the sentence.

Elizabeth didn't look at Bruce as he walked out the sliding glass door. Her wide eyes remained glued to Todd's face, but for the life of him he couldn't identify the emotion that lay behind them. Was it embarrassment? Remorse? Defiance?

Elizabeth took a hesitant step in Todd's direction. "Todd, I—"

He cut her off with a slicing hand gesture. "Don't," he snapped, his voice rough with anger and misery. "Save your breath. You don't need to explain—I've got eyes! You're in love . . ." Todd choked on the words. For a moment he just wanted to cry. The girl he loved more than anyone else in the entire world had fallen for another guy—what did she need to say? "You're in love with Patman," Todd managed, barely able to keep his tears at bay. "I should've known you had a pretty good reason for treating me like dirt all week!"

"In love with Bruce?" Elizabeth exclaimed. "Treating you like dirt? I'm not—I didn't . . ." She shook her head. "Todd, what just happened with Bruce—it wasn't the way it looked. He's in a lot of pain. I was only—"

Todd laughed harshly. "In a lot of pain—yeah, right. I bet it's painful making out with someone else's girlfriend!"

"Todd, I said it wasn't like that!" Elizabeth cried, her voice rising in frustration. "Are you even

169

listening? No, of course not. Why should you start now? Maybe if you hadn't been so self-absorbed all week, I wouldn't have had to turn to—"

"Oh, so now it's all my fault!" Todd spat. "How can you stand there, after what just happened, and accuse *me* of being selfish?"

"Because you *are* selfish! You won't let me explain, you won't give me the benefit of the doubt, you won't . . ." Elizabeth burst into tears. "You just won't let me *be*," she sobbed incoherently.

"Is that what you want?" Todd asked, a quaver in his voice. "You want me to let you be?" Elizabeth just stood, crying quietly. "Well, you've got it," Todd bit out, yanking the car keys from his pocket. "I hope you'll be happy now."

Elizabeth heard Todd slam the front door behind him. The sound echoed in her overheated, bewildered brain. She had a feeling she'd be hearing that door slam for a long time to come.

What just happened? Elizabeth wondered, turning on the sink faucet so she could splash cold water on her face. One moment she was kissing Bruce, and Todd was the furthest thing from her mind; the next moment there was Todd, and Elizabeth couldn't believe she'd been kissing Bruce. *Am I losing my mind?*

Elizabeth patted her face dry with a clean dish towel. Taking a deep breath, she picked up the platter of raw vegetables and walked over to the

170

sliding glass door. *My world may be falling apart, but I'm giving a party,* she reminded herself. *I can't hide in the kitchen all night.*

But there was something else she knew she couldn't do. She couldn't deal with either Bruce or Todd. *Todd's gone, so I just have to avoid Bruce,* Elizabeth thought, ducking back into the crowd by the pool and hoping that the dim light masked any lingering traces of tears.

"Elizabeth."

The soft, familiar voice stopped Elizabeth in her tracks. Turning slowly, she mustered a half-hearted smile. "Pamela, hi. How's it going?"

"Actually . . ." Pamela shifted her feet. Her blue eyes were rimmed with red, and Elizabeth guessed why she had sought her out. "Can I talk to you for a minute?" Pamela asked.

"Sure," Elizabeth said as she put the vegetable platter down on a snack table.

They walked together to the side lawn, out of sight of the pool party. In the shadowy moonlight, Pamela looked fragile. "I just wanted to tell you," she began, "Bruce and I—we broke up."

Elizabeth gasped. "Oh, Pamela, I'm so—"

Pamela held up a hand. "I know it's not your fault. You probably didn't mean for it to happen— you're not that type. But he's—he's fallen in love with you," she stammered, sniffling.

"In love with *me*?" Elizabeth repeated, wide-eyed. Her pale, heart-shaped face a picture of utter

171

grief, Pamela nodded. "I gave him his freedom—it was the only thing to do. I just thought you should know." Her voice dwindled to a whisper. "You two can be together now, if that's what you want."

Elizabeth was too stunned to speak. Pamela, not expecting a reply, had turned and fled like a ghost into the night, leaving Elizabeth alone in the shadows.

Bruce loves me? He broke up with Pamela because of me? Elizabeth didn't want to believe it, but she knew it was probably true. Their encounter in the kitchen hadn't been an accident; it was the culmination of a week of discovery, of longing. *Bruce kissed me and I kissed him back. Maybe we are falling in love.*

Elizabeth's legs crumpled and she sank down on the grass. Her head whirled with thoughts of Bruce and Todd, of her mother and Mr. Patman, of her mother and father—of love coming and going like the ocean tides . . .

What is love, anyway? Elizabeth wondered, her heart aching. She climbed wearily to her feet. A voice rose above the din of music and voices in the backyard.

"Burgers, everyone!" Jessica shouted.

As he rounded the bend, Todd stepped on the gas, and the BMW's engine hummed eagerly in response. Through the windows, the trees along the roadside streamed backward at astonishing speed.

172

Whoa, Todd said to himself, letting up on the gas and coasting until his speed dropped back down to the legal limit. Blowing off steam was one thing, risking his life was another.

At the next corner, he turned left—not for any reason. He'd been driving aimlessly around Sweet Valley for half an hour, and he was starting to think he'd be at it all night. *I'll never calm down,* Todd thought, sucking in deep breaths of warm night air and trying hard not to cry. *And I'll never understand her.*

"What does she want, anyway?" he asked out loud, pounding the steering wheel in frustration. "Why does she push me away every time I try to get close? And why did she have to dump me for Bruce Patman, out of all the guys in Sweet Valley?"

By the time he'd done three laps of the Secca Lake access road, Todd was starting to cool down. *Okay, maybe I overreacted when I caught her with Bruce,* he reflected. *But we've been bickering for days. Whose fault is that?*

Mulling it over, Todd reluctantly had to admit to himself that it was at least partly *his* fault that he and Elizabeth hadn't been seeing eye to eye. Whether it's working well or falling apart, it takes two people to have a relationship, he acknowledged. *And that's what I was pushing for—more togetherness and all that. But Elizabeth . . . obviously she needed something else.*

This isn't the first time I didn't listen to her,

Todd realized, remembering the night of the Jungle Prom a few months earlier. Elizabeth's behavior had been really out of character—she'd totally cut loose, dancing up a storm and hanging all over Jessica's boyfriend, Sam. Todd had judged her harshly, but as it turned out, Elizabeth had had a serious problem: her punch had been spiked and she'd gotten very drunk. *I didn't listen then and I haven't been listening this time, either,* Todd realized. *I've been handling things all wrong. I've made it hard instead of easy for her to confide in me, to let me in on what's going on inside of her.*

Pulling over on the side of the road, Todd sat in the car with the engine idling, gazing pensively at the still, moonlit lake. "I just assumed living together would automatically make us closer," he mused aloud. "I was so busy laying out my own agenda, I didn't even consider her feelings."

Slumping in his seat, Todd pressed his hands against his skull, trying to erase the picture of Elizabeth kissing Bruce. It was just too painful. Then he sat up straight. It was painful because he loved Elizabeth with all his heart. He loved her too much just to hand her over to Bruce without a fight.

Shifting into first gear, Todd steered the BMW off the shoulder and back onto the access road. His jaw set and his eyes bright, he headed back toward Elizabeth's. *This time, I'm going to talk with her instead of at her,* Todd determined. *This time, I'm going to listen.*

Elizabeth walked around the perimeter of the patio, keeping to the fringes of the party so she wouldn't have to talk to anybody. *I wish they'd all leave,* she thought, glowering at the horde of laughing, yelling, splashing kids playing volleyball at one end of the pool.

"Elizabeth, there you are!" Jessica squealed, hurdling over a chaise lounge in an attempt to ambush her sister. Gripping Elizabeth's arm, she gave it an excited shake. "Liz, the whole party's buzzing. Jeanie said she overheard Bruce talking to Pamela, and Amy saw Pamela talking to *you,* and Caroline . . ." Jessica could hardly get the words out, she was so worked up. "Caroline just happened to be standing near the window when you were in the kitchen with Bruce, and Todd walked in!"

"Caroline just happened to be standing by the window," Elizabeth said in disgust. "God, don't these people have anything better to do?"

"Of course not!" Jessica hadn't relinquished her grip on her sister's arm, and now she gave it an insistent squeeze. "Well, is it true?" she demanded. "Are you and Bruce the hottest new couple at Sweet Valley High?"

"I don't know what we are," Elizabeth snapped. She peeled Jessica's fingers off her arm. "Just leave me alone, okay?"

Before Jessica could grab her again, Elizabeth turned to flee. "I was just trying to get the story straight," Jessica called after her. "Don't blame me if you end up being crushed by the rumor mill!"

Right now, gossip was the least of Elizabeth's worries. What did it matter what other people said when she herself wasn't even sure what happened? *Maybe I'll just go inside,* Elizabeth thought. *I'll lock my bedroom door and—*

"Elizabeth Wakefield. I've been looking all over for you!"

Elizabeth turned to see Enid slip away from the crowd. "I heard that you and Todd had a fight. Do you want to go sit someplace quiet and talk?" Enid offered, her green eyes warm with concern.

Enid's gentle voice and manner were a direct contrast to Jessica's, but for some reason Elizabeth didn't want to have this conversation either. At some point, she'd dump her latest troubles on Enid and get her advice, but just then Elizabeth didn't want to talk about Bruce or Todd or *anything* to anyone. "Thanks, Enid, but I just can't, not now—it's still too fresh."

She scurried away before Enid could respond. *Where can I go?* Elizabeth wondered, looking around the backyard desperately. *Where can I go to get away from the eyes, the voices, the questions?*

Her gaze settled on the swimming pool. The volleyball game had moved up onto the lawn, and the water was blue and calm and inviting. *I'll take a swim,* Elizabeth decided. Pivoting, she walked briskly toward the pool. She wanted to feel the cool water slide over her skin and wash away her pain. Underwater, she wouldn't have to hear or see anyone.

Tossing her sarong aside, Elizabeth hopped up onto the diving board and strode to the end. One, two, three . . . She bounced higher and higher, the blood flowing fizzy and fast through her veins. *Todd,* Elizabeth thought, taking a hard bounce. She bounced again. *Bruce.*

Just a few more bounces, and then she'd dive. *Todd, Bruce, Todd, Bruce . . .*

Taking one last bounce, Elizabeth sprang into the air.

Too high, she realized suddenly as her body soared upward, folded into a jackknife, and pointed straight down like an arrow. *I'll hit the bottom,* she thought. Panicking, she tried to flatten out her dive, but it was too late. . . .

Jessica was back at the grill, flipping burgers, when the figure of someone bouncing on the diving board caught her attention. "Elizabeth knows better than that," Jessica murmured. "You can't bounce that high—the water's not deep enough. How many times did Mom and Dad tell us when we were growing up . . . ?"

Jessica was about to shout out a warning when Elizabeth sprang from the board. At the height of the dive, her flawless, graceful elegance was suddenly perverted as Elizabeth realized her mistake.

She came down hard in the water, in a flop that looked as painful as it must have felt.

Jessica held her breath, waiting for her sister to resurface. But the water remained smooth and unbroken, and at the bottom of the pool, Jessica saw something dark and unmoving.

"Elizabeth!" Jessica screamed, tossing the spatula aside and racing toward the pool. "Somebody help Elizabeth! *Hurry!*"

Chapter 16

Todd parked his car on the street and cut across the Wakefields' lawn just as Jessica's terrified scream shattered the night.

His heart in his throat, Todd sprinted toward the swimming pool, kicking off his sneakers as he went. Kids were shouting and gesturing; some guy stood poised to jump in after her. But Todd beat him to it. His gaze fixed on the limp form at the bottom of the pool, he took one final stride and dove into the water, aiming his body like an arrow.

His arms stroked strongly, shoving the water aside as he fought his way to the bottom of the pool. Chlorine stinging his eyes, his lungs bursting, Todd reached forward. He touched her.

Hooking one arm around Elizabeth's body, Todd kicked back to the surface. Hands reached down from the side of the pool, dragging him and Elizabeth up onto the deck.

Todd bent over Elizabeth's limp, dripping body. For a gut-wrenching, eternal moment, he feared he'd reached her too late. Her eyes were closed, and she lay impossibly still. *Come on, Elizabeth,* he prayed silently. *You've got to breathe. You can't be . . .*

Suddenly Elizabeth's eyelids fluttered. Her body convulsing, she coughed the water up from her lungs.

"She's OK!" Winston shouted.

Todd cradled Elizabeth in his arms, lifting her shoulders so she could breathe more easily. She blinked up at him, a wondering expression on her face.

They were surrounded by anxious friends, but for Todd they were the only two people on earth. "Elizabeth," Todd murmured thankfully, tears of relief springing to his eyes. He held her closer to him. "You're safe now."

With an effort, Elizabeth focused on the face looking down at her, the face of the boy holding her in warm, strong arms. "Todd," she whispered, coughing again. "Todd, is that you?"

"Yes. It's me." She felt a gentle hand smooth her wet, tangled hair back from her forehead. "I'm here."

A convulsive shiver wracked Elizabeth's body.

"Here," said Jessica, kneeling down next to Todd and Elizabeth and wrapping a thick terry-cloth beach towel around her sister.

"She's had the wind knocked out of her, but she's all right," Enid called out to everyone now hovering over Elizabeth and Todd. "Just clear out of the way and give her some air."

Todd's arms tightened around Elizabeth and she felt him lift her onto a lounge chair. He continued to hold her and to gaze hungrily into her eyes as if he were seeing her for the first time.

No one but Todd could look at me that way. Slowly Elizabeth's thoughts untangled themselves and she saw things clearly, as if the great cloud blocking her view had finally moved aside. *No one but Todd could love me so wholeheartedly.*

"I'm so sorry," Elizabeth whispered. "I'm sorry I treated you badly. Can you ever forgive me?"

"Oh, Elizabeth, I'm the one who should be sorry. I've been totally insensitive, and—" Todd's voice broke with emotion and he pressed her close to his heart. "In the pool, when I thought you were . . . I don't think I could have gone on living without you. I love you, Elizabeth."

"I love you, too," she said, her eyes brimming with tears. "I never stopped loving you. I was just confused."

"Of course you were," said Todd. "I should have seen that—I should have understood."

"I didn't give you a chance to understand," Elizabeth admitted. "I just assumed you couldn't. I felt so mixed up. About relationships, you know? Mine, Mom's . . . As for Bruce . . ." The scene in the kitchen already felt as if it had taken place in another lifetime.

Todd waited patiently for her to complete her sentence. "Bruce and I made a mistake," Elizabeth said at last, her voice steady. "We got carried away looking into the past—we were caught up in our parents' love story. But whatever happened back then, and whatever may be happening now, that's their story, not ours. Bruce and I have to live our own lives, and just because our parents may have this connection, it doesn't mean Bruce and I are meant to be together too." Elizabeth cupped Todd's face in her hands and gazed deeply into his eyes, her own eyes shining. "I'm meant to be with *you*, Todd Wilkins."

Gently Todd pulled her to him. As his lips touched Elizabeth's, the love that flowed from their hearts enveloped them both like a warm blanket.

The party had quieted down; people clustered together at a polite distance from Elizabeth and Todd, talking in low voices. Alone, Bruce stood in the shadows at the edge of the lawn, watching the tender reunion from afar.

He couldn't hear what Elizabeth and Todd were saying to each other, but their gestures spoke louder than words. Todd stroked Elizabeth's hair, she touched his face, they held each other close, they kissed. . . .

"You are the world's biggest fool, Patman," Bruce said out loud. He shook his head, amazed at the state of mind he'd been in just minutes before. *For a while there, I actually believed Liz Wakefield and I were right for each other. I must have been out of my mind.*

It was pretty apparent that despite recent events, at this moment Elizabeth Wakefield and Todd Wilkins were still what they'd always been: the steadiest, most-committed couple in the junior class. *She got a little sidetracked, maybe, but Wilkins is the one she's wild about,* Bruce had to acknowledge. *She would've come to her senses sooner or later.*

We have absolutely zilch in common, he remembered, trying to rationalize his pain. *We're polar opposites in the personality department. If it weren't for the fact that our parents are having an affair, we'd probably have nothing to talk about.*

Our parents . . . The insight hit Bruce like a ton of bricks. *I convinced myself I was falling in love with Elizabeth because I wanted to see in her what Dad saw—sees in her mother. And I wanted Elizabeth to see me the way her mom sees Dad.*

Bruce kicked at the grass with a dejected sigh. The more he thought about his behavior that week, the more deluded and pathetic it seemed. He'd been chasing after a phantom while turning his back on the one person who might really have helped him through this difficult time. Pamela, who'd run home crying. Pamela, who might never want to see or talk to him again.

How did things get so crazy and complicated? Bruce wondered, lying down on the grass and looking up at the stars.

"This is like one of those reality TV shows," Jessica gushed, tagging along as Todd carried Elizabeth into the house and up the stairs. "Elizabeth crashes into the pool and has the wind knocked out of her, and Todd jumps in to make a heroic rescue and saves her from certain death. Wow. I wish I could have gotten it on tape. Hey, Liz, I don't suppose you'd consider reenacting the part where—"

"Jessica, you are too much," Elizabeth groaned as Todd set her down on her feet in her bedroom. "The only scene I'm going to reenact now is the one I do every night: brushing my teeth and going to bed."

"I was only kidding." Jessica held out her sister's bathrobe so Elizabeth could slip her arms into the sleeves. "Tell you what," she said in a motherly tone. "Why don't you take a long, steamy shower, and I'll run down and make you a pot of hot tea. Then Todd and I will tuck you in nice and cozy."

Elizabeth gave her sister a grateful smile. "Don't worry about the tea. Get back to the party. It's still early—you don't want everybody to think it's over, do you?"

Elizabeth had a point. *Todd can take care of her,* Jessica thought. *Now that they're all lovey-dovey again.* "Okay," Jessica agreed. "Let me know if you need anything," she called over her shoulder as she stepped into the hall. "Otherwise, I'll see you guys in the morning. And, Todd, I'll probably sleep late, but waking up to waffles might be nice."

"Yeah, the frozen kind you can pop in the toaster yourself," Todd quipped.

Laughing, Jessica turned to head for the stairs . . . and stopped dead in her tracks. She clapped a hand to her mouth, her eyes widening as she realized who it was. *"Mom!"* she yelped.

Mrs. Wakefield greeted her daughter with a tight smile. "I guess I surprised you," she said dryly. "Or is this party for me?"

Oh, man, are we in major-league trouble! Jessica adopted her most abjectly apologetic expression, hoping to forestall retribution. "We just invited a few people over," she swore, backing into Elizabeth's bedroom so her sister could take part of the rap. "I guess word got around, though—you know how it is. All of a sudden there was this whole *mob*. What could we do?"

Close behind Jessica, Mrs. Wakefield reached the doorway to Elizabeth's bedroom and then stopped, folding her arms across her chest. *She's not even listening to me,* Jessica thought, puzzled. She glanced at Elizabeth and Todd, who'd jumped apart guiltily. Looking back at her mother, it wasn't

185

hard to guess what was coming next. *Somebody is about to get in trouble,* Jessica anticipated, *and for once, it's not going to be me!*

Todd cleared his throat. "Uh, hi, Mrs. Wakefield."

"Hi, Mom," Elizabeth squeaked. "You're home early!"

Alice Wakefield tapped her foot on the carpet, something she only did, Jessica knew, when she was *very* mad. "Yes, I am," she said flatly. "I decided I didn't really need to be present at the wrap-up brunch meeting scheduled for tomorrow and I'd rather get home to my children."

"That—that's nice," Elizabeth stuttered.

"Isn't it?" Mrs. Wakefield's foot tapped faster. "Well, as I hiked home just now after parking my car about half a mile away because I couldn't get into my own driveway, I bumped into the Beckwiths walking their dog. They had some interesting news for me."

Todd dropped his eyes and shuffled his feet, looking as if he wanted to turn and jump out the window. Elizabeth gulped. Lurking behind her mother in the doorway, Jessica grinned. *What an intriguing turn of events. Elizabeth is in the hot seat for a change,* she thought, enjoying the scene immensely.

"According to the Beckwiths," Mrs. Wakefield continued, "they were concerned when they noticed a strange car parked in our driveway at all

186

hours of the day and night. They stopped worrying, however, when they realized it was *Todd's* car."

"Todd's been spending a lot of time here," Elizabeth conceded.

"I gathered that," Mrs. Wakefield snapped, "when I saw the duffel bag in the den and the shaving kit in the bathroom."

Elizabeth's cheeks flamed red, and for once, she was at a total loss for words. Jessica darted to her sister's side. "Mom, don't be too hard on her," she begged, putting a supportive arm around Elizabeth. "She almost *drowned* just now!"

"What?" Mrs. Wakefield's expression changed instantly from anger to anxiety. "What happened? Are you all right, Elizabeth?"

"I'm fine," Elizabeth assured her. "I messed up on a dive and hit the water belly first. I swallowed some water and blacked out for a few seconds, but Todd pulled me out."

"Oh my goodness!" Mrs. Wakefield rushed forward to run her hands gently over Elizabeth's head. "My poor baby!"

"Mom, I'm fine," Elizabeth reiterated. "Really."

Mrs. Wakefield stepped back with an exasperated sigh. "I just don't know what to do with you kids!" she exclaimed. "Elizabeth, I'm surprised at you. I can't believe that you would take advantage of a situation to do something you know your father and I would never allow. And what would *your* parents think about this, Todd?"

187

Todd hung his head. "I don't think they'd be too psyched."

Mrs. Wakefield laughed dryly. "I'd say that's an understatement." Her patent-leather pump started tapping again. *Good*, Jessica thought. *For a minute there, I thought she was going to let Liz off the hook!*

"I thought we had a better relationship," Mrs. Wakefield went on, fixing Elizabeth with a sorrowful gaze. "I thought I could trust you to be responsible. To think you'd go behind my back like this! I can't tell you how disappointed I am."

Elizabeth's shoulders had started to slump; Jessica knew it pained her sister immensely to be lectured this way. *Mommy's little angel*, Jessica thought with amusement. *Miss Goody Two-Shoes, caught having sleepovers with her boyfriend!*

But her mother's final statement seemed to trigger something in Elizabeth. She sat up straight, her eyes flashing. "*You're* disappointed in me, Mom?" she countered hotly. "What about the sneaking around *you've* been doing?"

Todd's jaw dropped. Jessica gaped at Elizabeth in utter disbelief. Mrs. Wakefield blinked.

Elizabeth sprang to her feet, her hands on her hips, and stared her mother straight in the eye. "What about your marriage to Mr. Patman?" Elizabeth pressed. "And what about room four forty-four at the Drake Hotel?"

Chapter 17

Elizabeth's accusation hung in the air, echoing over and over. As Elizabeth watched in dread, all color drained from her mother's face, leaving her delicate skin as white as paper. *She can't deny it. She's guilty,* Elizabeth thought, her heart galloping like a runaway horse.

The words had just spilled out before Elizabeth had a chance to think about what she was saying. Now she wished more than anything that she could take them back. *I really don't want to know,* she realized. *It already hurts too much.* But it was too late. Ready or not, they were going to learn the truth.

Mrs. Wakefield drew a deep breath. "I was never married to Henry Patman," she stated.

"Don't lie to us, Mom," Elizabeth cried. "I saw your wedding picture. And your dress. Bruce and I found the wedding rings in a trunk in his attic," she continued breathlessly. "And Mrs. Patman walked out on Mr. Patman because he's having an affair. And then you and he went to Chicago on business together. And—and—" Elizabeth's voice broke on a sob. Todd slipped an arm around her trembling shoulders. "It all adds up. You can't deny it!"

"Ah, the rings and the photograph." The puzzled wrinkle in Mrs. Wakefield's forehead disappeared. She looked remarkably calm, Elizabeth thought, for someone whose back was against the wall. "Well, I guess I owe you an explanation," her mother said. "Todd, would you see if you can find Bruce, please? He should hear this too."

Five minutes later they'd regrouped in the living room. Elizabeth and Bruce sat stiffly at opposite ends of the sofa, with Jessica in between them. Todd took an armchair facing Mrs. Wakefield across the coffee table.

Mrs. Wakefield crossed her legs and leaned forward, her elbows on her knees. "I told the others that I was never married to your father," she began, addressing Bruce. "And that's the truth. But I can understand your confusion, given all the evidence to the contrary. Let me explain.

"Hank Patman and I met when we were in college. He was older than me, and quite a big man on campus. And he was handsome. In fact, he looked a lot like you do now." She smiled at Bruce. "Never-

190

theless, when he first asked me out, I wasn't interested. I was kind of a flower child." She laughed. "Long hair, peace symbols embroidered all over my clothes, very eager to change the world, which I suppose I still am, but in a different way. I thought Hank was rich, spoiled, arrogant, and totally out of touch."

Bruce raised his eyebrows quizzically. "Well, wasn't he?"

Mrs. Wakefield smiled. "Let's just say he surprised me, and a lot of other people too. He turned out to have some pretty diverse interests. We found ourselves working for some of the same causes, and after the administration sit-in, when he dropped the food from the helicopter, I guess we fell in love."

"Undying love," Elizabeth whispered, remembering the sentiment engraved on the rings she and Bruce had found.

Out of the corner of her eye, Elizabeth saw Bruce turn his head sharply.

"What was that?" Mrs. Wakefield asked.

Elizabeth looked down at her hands. "Nothing."

"So, what happened next?" Jessica demanded.

"Hank swept me off my feet," Mrs. Wakefield admitted, some of the color returning to her cheeks. "He was very gallant and attentive. And persistent! Dates, flowers, and finally a beautiful diamond ring. We became engaged to be married."

"But you were so young!" Elizabeth couldn't help

exclaiming. "How could you have been so sure he was the one?"

"That's just the point," her mother said. "Hank was a wonderful guy, and he wanted to marry me, and it seemed like a dream come true. But the whole time we were engaged, deep down in my heart, there were some doubts. And I didn't really acknowledge them until I met someone else."

"Dad!" Jessica shouted.

"Yes, Ned Wakefield," Mrs. Wakefield confirmed. "Did I ever tell you girls about the first time I met your father?"

Elizabeth and Jessica shook their heads.

"I was at the beach with Hank and some of his friends." Mrs. Wakefield's lips twisted in a wry smile. "Maybe that's why I didn't tell you! Anyway, I went for a swim in the ocean, and as I started back toward shallow water, I cramped up and went under. A surfer who'd been watching me from the shore swam out to my rescue. If it weren't for him, I would have died that day."

"Dad!" Jessica cried out again.

"Dad saved you from drowning?" Elizabeth said, astonished.

Her mother nodded. "We became friends, and one day he asked me out. But when I told him I was engaged to someone else, he backed off. It didn't matter that I hardly ever saw him. From that day on, I couldn't get Ned Wakefield out of my head."

"But you were going to marry Hank!" Jessica protested.

Mrs. Wakefield shrugged. "All I can say in my own defense is that I realized the mistake I was about to make *before* I actually made it. The wedding was to be at the Patman mansion. Your house, Bruce." Elizabeth shot a glance at Bruce, who looked as if he were about to burst from the tension and suspense. "The day came, and it was beautiful. All our friends and relatives had gathered. We posed for pictures, and at the very last minute, I realized that, as good a man as he was, we didn't have enough in common to make a life together."

Elizabeth sat paralyzed and speechless, her eyes as wide as saucers. Jessica, meanwhile, bounced on the sofa as though it were a trampoline. "Mom, what did you do?" she panted breathlessly.

"I ran," Mrs. Wakefield said simply. "In my wedding dress, I ran all the way to . . . all the way home. Maybe it was cowardly, but I didn't know what else to do."

"It wasn't cowardly, Mom. It was brave," Elizabeth said softly.

Mrs. Wakefield looked into her daughter's eyes. "Thanks, honey."

"Wow." Bruce wilted back against the sofa like a popped balloon. "My dad must have been totally crushed."

"That was the hard part," Mrs. Wakefield admitted. "I really hurt his feelings. And his pride. But he got over it. We both got over it. It was a chapter in our lives that we both decided, tacitly, to keep a secret."

"You married other people," said Elizabeth.

"We did. And though they may be having some troubles now, I know for certain that Hank was much happier with Marie than he ever could have been with me," Mrs. Wakefield said firmly. "And I was happier with Ned. Things worked out for the best."

Elizabeth looked from Todd to Bruce and back again. Once again, she found herself feeling very close to the girl her mother had been many years ago. *Just like Mom, I fell for the Patman charm,* Elizabeth thought. She smiled at Todd, her eyes shining. *But when it came to the test, I also knew the real thing.*

"Wow," Bruce muttered again, still trying to digest everything he'd just heard. It was tough to reconcile the twins' down-to-earth mother with the image of a runaway bride, but the story rang true. *Dad got ditched at the altar!* Bruce thought, a jubilant smile wreathing his face. *Alice Robertson got cold feet and took off. Mom was the one and only Mrs. Patman!*

Bruce's smile faded and his shoulders slumped again. And she was about to become his father's "ex."

There was still one question Mrs. Wakefield hadn't answered. But for his life, Bruce couldn't bring himself to ask it.

On the other end of the couch, though, Elizabeth appeared to be thinking along the same lines.

"You and Mr. Patman never actually got married, I get that part," Elizabeth said. She licked her lips nervously. "But what about now?"

A shadow crossed her mother's face. "It breaks my heart that you believe I would do anything to hurt your father, or this family," Mrs. Wakefield said, her eyes on Elizabeth and Jessica. "Hank Patman and I are not having an affair, nor will we ever have one! We were in love once, but that's over now. We are business associates. That's all there is to it. Actually, these past few weeks have really been a treat. Working closely together on this project has enabled us to become good friends again, after all these years."

"What about room four forty-four at the Drake?" Jessica prodded.

"Boy, you kids don't miss a trick, do you?" Mrs. Wakefield shook her head ruefully. "Room four forty-four at the Drake Hotel in Chicago is a two-bedroom, two-bath suite with an adjoining living room for entertaining clients."

Jessica grinned. "Did you order room service together? See Hank in his pajamas?"

Elizabeth hit her sister with a throw pillow. All the questions had been answered, all the fears put to rest; everyone in the room seemed to breathe a sigh of relief. Everyone, that is, except Bruce.

Sure, it's great that Dad was never married to Mrs. Wakefield, he thought glumly. *And he's not having an affair with her now—that's great too.*

195

But that just means he's probably having an affair with someone else.

Bruce looked up to find Mrs. Wakefield's sympathetic eyes resting on his face. "Bruce, I'm sorry about what you and Roger and your parents are going through. But you shouldn't give up hope. Sometimes a marriage reaches a crisis, but that doesn't mean it's over for good. Anything could happen."

"Yeah, anything," Bruce agreed morosely. "Like a divorce." He felt a gentle hand touch his shoulder. Turning, he saw that Elizabeth had reached behind Jessica to give him a comfortable squeeze. For a moment, they just looked quietly into each other's eyes. A silent understanding passed between them. *We were never really in love, but we were friends,* their eyes communicated. *And we'll stay friends.*

Elizabeth turned back to her mother. "Now that we've solved the mystery, we still have a puzzle to work on. We have to get Bruce's parents back together!"

"That would be wonderful," Mrs. Wakefield agreed.

"There's no way." Bruce shook his head dejectedly. "Things have gone too far. My mom moved out."

"I didn't say it would be easy," Elizabeth conceded. "But it's worth a shot, don't you think, Mom? Because maybe, just the way you and Hank getting married would've been a mistake, Marie and Hank getting un-married might be a mistake."

"Well, it's worth a shot," Mrs. Wakefield said. "We need a strategy, though."

"Right. A plan," Elizabeth murmured thoughtfully.

Instinctively she, Bruce, Todd, and Mrs. Wakefield all turned to the best schemer they knew. "How 'bout it, Jessica?" they said in unison.

"Think you can do it?" Bruce asked hopefully.

"I'd be honored," Jessica said proudly.

"I should probably head home," Todd whispered to Elizabeth later that night.

The pool party was over, and a warm, quiet darkness had settled over the Wakefield house and yard. Jessica and Mrs. Wakefield had gone to bed; Elizabeth and Todd sat on the front steps with Todd's duffel bag, packed and ready to be tossed into the trunk of the BMW, at their feet.

Elizabeth hooked her arm through Todd's and rested her head on his shoulder. "Stay just a minute longer," she pleaded. "It's been such a crazy night—such a crazy week. This feels so nice and normal, though. I don't want you to leave yet."

"Should I unpack my duffel?" he teased.

Elizabeth smiled up at him. "Not on your life!"

Slinging an arm around her shoulders, Todd gave her a squeeze. "That's what's so nice and normal about this—we're dating again, not living together."

"Right," Elizabeth agreed happily.

For a few minutes they sat in companionable silence, enjoying the peaceful beauty of the night.

The thunderstorm that had threatened earlier had retreated. *I guess the heat wave's not over after all,* Elizabeth observed. She didn't really mind. Another steamy morning might wait over the horizon, but at this moment, with a balmy breeze ruffling her hair and moonshadows dancing on the front lawn, she thought the weather was fine.

"You know, I think it was worth it. This whole living-together experiment," Elizabeth said thoughtfully. "We thought it was just a game, you know? That it would be easy, like in the Beach Boys song. But finding out about my mom and Mr. Patman, Bruce's parents splitting up, worrying that *my* parents were going to be next . . . all of that made me think that this is serious stuff. I'm not ready to pretend I'm married! I think I just got scared and had to back off from you."

"I guess it was too much, too soon," Todd conceded. "We didn't really know what we were getting into." He grinned. "And I don't mean the soap suds at the Videomat! We should've taken the time to talk about our expectations."

"Next time," Elizabeth said with a smile.

"Next time?" Todd asked eagerly. "We can still look forward to the future, right?"

Turning, Elizabeth wrapped her arms around her boyfriend's waist. She gazed deeply into his eyes, just as she had after he pulled her from the swimming pool, saving her life. *This must be what Mom saw in Dad's eyes that very first day on the beach when* he *saved* her, Elizabeth thought. Strength, courage, integrity, generosity, humor, understanding, devotion . . . love.

"I think we can look forward to a very long future together," Elizabeth whispered, just as Todd's mouth met hers in a kiss.

Don't miss Sweet Valley High #103, **Operation Love Match***, the exciting conclusion to this three-part miniseries. Jessica, Elizabeth, and Bruce plot to get Bruce's parents back together and the result is disastrous!*

Bantam Books in the Sweet Valley High series
Ask your bookseller for the books you have missed

SIGN UP FOR THE
SWEET VALLEY HIGH®
FAN CLUB!

Hey, girls! Get all the gossip on Sweet
Valley High's® most popular teenagers
when you join our fantastic Fan Club!
As a member, you'll get all of this really
cool stuff:

- Membership Card with your own
  personal Fan Club ID number
- A Sweet Valley High® Secret
  Treasure Box
- Sweet Valley High® Stationery
- Official Fan Club Pencil (for secret
  note writing!)
- Three Bookmarks
- A "Members Only" Door Hanger
- Two Skeins of J. & P. Coats® Embroidery
  Floss with flower barrette instruction
  leaflet
- Two editions of *The Oracle* newsletter
- Plus exclusive Sweet Valley High®
  product offers, special savings,
  contests, and much more!

Be the first to find out what Jessica & Elizabeth Wakefield are up to by joining the
Sweet Valley High® Fan Club for the one-year membership fee of only $6.25 each
for U.S. residents, $8.25 for Canadian residents (U.S. currency). Includes shipping
& handling.

Send a check or money order (do not send cash) made payable to "Sweet Valley
High® Fan Club" along with this form to:

SWEET VALLEY HIGH® FAN CLUB, BOX 3919-B, SCHAUMBURG, IL 60168-3919

NAME_____
(Please print clearly)

ADDRESS_____

CITY_____ STATE _____ ZIP_____
(Required)

AGE_____ BIRTHDAY_____ /_____ /_____